Blood Test

Syracuse University Press and the

King Fahd Center for Middle East and Islamic Studies,

University of Arkansas,

are pleased to announce BLOOD TEST *as the 2007 Winner*

of the King Fahd Center for Middle East and Islamic Studies

Translation of Arabic Literature Award

Blood Test

A NOVEL

· · ·

Abbas Beydoun

Translated from the Arabic by Max Weiss

SYRACUSE UNIVERSITY PRESS

English translation copyright © 2008 by Syracuse University Press

Syracuse, New York 13244-5160

All Rights Reserved

First Edition 2008

08 09 10 11 12 13   6 5 4 3 2 1

Originally published as *Tahleel dam* (Beirut: Riyad el-Rayyes, 2002).

The paper used in this publication meets the minimum requirements of
American National Standard for Information Sciences—Permanence of
Paper for Printed Library Materials, ANSI Z39.48–1984.∞™

For a listing of books published and distributed by Syracuse University Press,
visit our Web site at SyracuseUniversityPress.syr.edu.

ISBN-13: 978-0-8156-0912-4   ISBN-10: 0-8156-0912-4

LIBRARY OF CONGRESS CATALOGING-IN-PUBLICATION DATA

Baydun, 'Abbas.

[Tahlil dam. English]

Blood test : a novel / Abbas Beydoun ; translated from the Arabic by Max Weiss. — 1st ed.

p. cm.

ISBN 978-0-8156-0912-4 (pbk. : alk. paper)

I. Weiss, Max. II. Title.

PJ7816.A928T3413 2008

892.7—dc22

2008034026

Manufactured in the United States of America

Blood Test

I wasn't surprised to find my aunt fuming behind the door because when she is upset, repellent expressions come out of her mouth: the whore. The seventy-year-old virgin used to scream with her head held back and make her nose into that hideous lump that is now in my face. I hated her in those moments. It was clear that the woman sitting in the courtyard wasn't saying much to my mother. She was dazed, dressed in a gray robe that was about the same color as her dark face, which seemed to have been stamped by another race. I didn't go near her, and she didn't notice me right away. My sister told me she was Safia, my uncle's fiancée. Twenty years later, especially ever since my father's death this fall, the mention of my uncle ceased to have any effect on me. For a long time, we guarded him like a secret. Then he disappeared, as all secrets do, without leaving a trace. My aunt came back from her house in Dakar with the dull kitchen knife, her skillets, and a large suitcase filled with his suits, shirts, neckties, and shaving kit. His clothes were too big for my brother. And my father, who had found in all this the opportunity to free himself from the memory of his brother, endured it in order to transcend his petrified pain, which had evolved over time into a silly and ineffable burden.

As the woman studied me, she said that I looked like my uncle. It seemed as if she said that only because she could no longer remember what he actually looked like. I had already heard from everyone else how I looked like my mother—which by itself was a good reason to loathe my face—and that my brother was the one who looked like my uncle. That's what my aunt said anyway, but after my brother died in a freak accident, she started saying I looked like him as well. Her descriptions always irritated me because I could tell she was lying to me about my own face, my own features, my own attributes. Still watching me, the woman conceded that I looked like my mother, too, and then turned her head to my mother, as if addressing her. For the first time, I noticed the length of her fingers and didn't even realize that I had been staring at her pursed lips, which were watery in a way that didn't quite match her dusty color. She chatted with my mother and me without mentioning my uncle again. I wondered where she knew my sister from, my sister who insisted on staying in her room and monitoring us through the window. My aunt was behind the door the whole time, and scandalous expressions were tumbling out of her mouth.

The stranger sat on the bench beside my father, and they both kept silent. He had my father's eyes and the same cleft in his chin that I had always considered my own private playground. I used to play with it when it had been freshly shaven, searching for the meaning of existence in that tiny indentation. There was another man on the bench, too, wearing an outfit that was something like cowboy-religious fusion, with a bony face and a cane by his side. He fumbled through his many pockets in search of a pack of cigarettes.

There was a semicircle around the bench. The women sat on the other side of the spacious room, which was the entire house, their long white veils draped over their shoulders, raising their hands and waving crumpled handkerchiefs that rested in their palms, dancing in their seats, repeatedly sitting down and then getting back up, communicating with their hands and heads—resembling birds in a cage. When the hanging lantern was obstructed, blackness suddenly replaced the luminous, swaying light, blanketing the men's side in darkness before the light suddenly returned to as it was, suspended over the middle of the room, forcing the women back out of it, and settling once again over the men's silence, dividing the racket made by some from the silence of others.

All this with barely a sound. Nothing but the doleful mourning and weeping of devastated young men. Nothing, that is, until a man's voice arose from the bench to recite a Qur'anic verse or exclaim an "Allahu Akbar," piercing a silence that no uproar or outcry seemed previously able to disturb. It was as though women were the shouters and men were the speakers. In this way, each and every word distinctly reached the opposite side of the room even though we couldn't make out anything else among this mixture of crying, chanting, broken sentences, and jargon coated with the clamor rising from the women's side.

In any event, everything just washed over my mother, who sat with her *niqab* draped over the shoulders of her coat, which she hung onto for just such occasions, regardless of the season in which they might take place. She was unable to participate in their rituals—their wailing and their dancing—so she stayed where she was, shaking her head repeatedly, wracked with grief, uncertain of whether all this was happening for her benefit. Although the man was her husband's brother, she didn't feel as if she had ever really known him, even as those other women participated on behalf of someone they didn't actually know at all. The male voices that had been reciting Qur'anic verses or prayers for the Prophet one after another died down and became a droning that gradually melted into my exhaustion. My father's voice was crystal clear above this din, even though I couldn't make out exactly what he was saying. Crystal clear: just what I needed to fall asleep. Through a dust-dappled sunbeam, I spotted a large butterfly float in and flutter past the light bulb: large, bloodred, it flew into the darkness before darting at the light like an arrow. Everyone fell silent, their eyes transfixed on the light. Just then, a clump of dirt fell from the ceiling and onto the ground without making a sound. Confusion spread as if once again a secret had been revealed. Then the conversation and the wailing resumed all at once.

My mother said that my father didn't sleep that night or the night after; he waited until the house was empty, until we all had gone to sleep, to sit on the bench by himself and cry. The stranger came back the next morning and shared his awful news. My mother said that while everyone else was asleep, my father sat and yowled like a bull. I never once saw him in such a state. I couldn't sleep after she swore to me that he was only hanging on by the thinnest of threads. I wasn't able to sleep after she solemnly informed me how the doctor had warned her that her heart was like the glass of a light bulb—it couldn't withstand the slightest pressure. I would always get distracted listening to her describe people as having faces dry enough to crumble in their hands. Her descriptions made me nervous, so I simply stopped listening. I was offended by what she said about my father yowling like a bull. I didn't believe it even though the description got lodged in my head. The lowing of some loathsome bull overshadowed my father's body. I saw it—with such distaste—crooked, disfigured. Distortion has this unusual power: to disrupt our perceptions to the point that we can only regard ourselves in horror, until we are overtaken by its power, feeling some sort of hatred we had never noticed was there, hatred of people we thought we liked. There was a certain amount of hatred in my mother's parables that was no different. I felt her hatred toward me, toward my father. The truth of the matter is that my father didn't cry. My mother was the one who cried, on more than one occasion, for a man she didn't even know. But my father was unable to cry. His tears stung him back then, too. He felt lumps in his eyes and a lump in his throat. He was dried up, bereft of even a single drop of moisture. As dry as if the news had sucked the last water droplet out of him. Was this sadness or the inability to be sad? It was something like the absence of imagination, the absence of thought, or the absence of sensation: harsh and desiccated. That was why he yelled, and when he yelled, his voice came out solid and dry. He yelled, suddenly feeling heartless. He yelled a lot, pounded his hands against his knees and against his head. He was transcending that unsadness, until he felt that the whole thing was ridiculous, absolutely ridiculous, and he wondered where those voices he heard were coming from. He tried his best to remember, but the name running through his memory wouldn't surface. Nothing moved in the settled night either. He was transcending his unsadness and the emptiness with which his soul responded to sadness. Emptiness—or something like fullness with rigidity, but without voice.

It took a long time for him to realize he lacked tears. He spent his childhood without noticing how he subjected his senses to this terrible distortion. A simple cold was enough to make his head totally blank. Anyone else might have opened his eyes with the dawn to allow life to become real for him from that point forward. But everything flowed from that giant spring in his head. It brimmed with words and images and just about anything you could think of. He was nourished by it and was never bored, not even for a moment. Enchanted: both sadness and joy would uplift him as though they were just images for him and nothing more. Even if his sense of hearing or smell stopped functioning properly, his body would remain his implement. With a certain move, one he never made, he would certainly have been capable of flying. *Was that a distorted kind of happiness?* he would ask himself later. It often took him a while to rediscover that he had no tears. He sometimes yearned for such pleasure, for tears that might elevate him a little, but he didn't realize he had that desire until sometime later. He didn't realize it on its own, but in relation to other things. He realized it all at once, along with everything. In the beginning, they considered it a strength, but he was light and knew much better, understanding that not tears alone, but something like life in all its complexity would eventually grind him down. He realized that all at once and wasn't bothered by it. He still felt safe. He had just started feeling the weight of his senses, his weakness. What outraged him even more was the fact that he had become increasingly self-aware. In those moments when his ability to smell himself increased, this recognition of his own odor really pissed him off.

From an early age, we understood that not crying was somehow equivalent to not sweating for us. We often believed that this meant our bodies were cleaner— we sometimes even boasted about it. But, then, what did cleanliness have to do with that cold virus going around all winter, only to vanish in the summertime, leaving us full of snot? Didn't that also result from the filthiness of the body? Or did all of the potential energy of unused tears migrate to some other gland? No one seemed to notice that the left side of my father's face was mangled by that early fall from the top of the stairs. They believed that the ringing in the boy's ears and the pain he suffered around midnight couldn't be ameliorated by warm oil because of his overall poor health. So they started a regimen of feeding him anything and everything that was bloodred, irrigating him with powerful blood in place of his weak, worthless blood. He discovered when he was young that his left eye had been totally damaged, that neither medicine nor glasses would ever be able to fix his vision. His eye dried up even as his nose and ears gushed with fluid. His face was pulverized, a latticework of canals on the inside, though his exterior appeared to be just fine.

They thus dealt with him, particularly his mother, like someone who was unable to fend for himself. He required lots of restoratives all the time—milk; rose water with the coagulated blood found in spleen and liver; varieties of broth: bone broth or meat and rice soup, all reddish from vegetables. All of those foods restored him to health or perhaps they restored all of him back to health. The women kept at it mercilessly, as though he wouldn't have survived a single hour with an empty stomach, as if he didn't have the power to persevere on his own. As far as they were concerned, his malnourishment was from the lack of vitality in the food he ate, a sign of chronic illness. He was emaciated. And what to make of it? Was it his tumble down the stairs? He certainly had been very high up, and there was no doubt that he had been crushed when he crashed onto the floor. Did they think that he wasn't recovering as he ought to or that his spirit had never returned to him after his body had tasted death? Just imagine. Did they figure that he had lost his strength in that resurrection, that he deserved to live by virtue of that sacrifice, but only as though he had been forgotten by death temporarily, that he was one of death's remainders? He still had the power of speech and was intelligent enough, but the dead are always more eloquent than the living.

6 Abbas Beydoun

Once he had rapidly grown stronger than his brother, the situation became much clearer. On the one hand, here was a perpetual survivor carrying the glow of his continuing endurance on his sleeve; on the other hand, here was a living monster that was never going to be satisfied.

My father wasn't concerned with the stoppage of his tears. That was the obvious price of his fall: people don't come back from hell with tears in their eyes. Nevertheless, at times he felt as if his palms were coming apart at the seams, as if he were crying through his skin. Such crying was painful for him. He felt imprisoned, brimming with sweat behind his pores, but unable to free himself to squeeze out those droplets. At those times, he used to think about the body as full of essences that never reveal themselves, about how the self was also full of such essences that never freed themselves or that could not be released. He always felt that tears, like sweat and urine, were bodily necessities. He probably attributed his copious sweat to the repression of his tears. He was very sweaty and smelly, and at any given moment his body seemed to be secreting something. His hesitation at taking off his shoes when other people were around was entirely justified because the stench that emanated from his socks clouded the air, just like the damp, citrusy odor of his sweat, which he noticed well before others did, if they even noticed it at all. He was rarely conscious of his need to cry, but he believed that pain without tears was noble and that the body eliminated pain more slowly that way.

One time, returning home after the teacher had beaten his hands with the tire iron, he noticed that the marks had completely disappeared from his palms. He marveled at how the sores had vanished without leaving a trace. He had been beaten for what seemed like no reason, for merely continuing his extended silence or for being head of the class, both overlooked and looked down upon. On the way home, he kept feeling that nothing could remove those blows from his body; the disappearance of the visible markings made those feelings worse. The blows penetrated deep inside his body, leaving no discernible marks on his skin. They burrowed inside his body, and the pain remained there, suspended, like his tears.

He didn't know what his mother sensed from him when he came inside, but water filled her eyes without her feeling a thing. Her eyes brimmed with tears instinctually. There was lots of water and voiceless crying, a quick downpour, and then her face and her eyes cleared up without her understanding what had just happened. At that moment, he became aware of the fact that she cried over things he conveyed to her. He became even more convinced of this transference when he noticed that dog chained up in the courtyard. He wouldn't have noticed it except that the dog let out a small, muffled yelp from behind him. He spun around to find the dog resting on his front legs, regarding him. It was no ordinary look. In those almond-shaped eyes, he saw the end of things, the end of torture as it is transformed into grace, the end of evil as it is transformed into kindness, the farewell that is followed by total oblivion. He looked at him and something sparkled. Without warning, he saw tears streaming from the dog's eyes.

When his father died, it rekindled a lifelong anxiety that he wouldn't be able to mourn his passing. He probably feared that deep down inside he somehow desired it, that he truly hungered for the death of all his relatives. Death was always a noble event. In his worst nightmares, he would awake after seeing himself crowned by it: the death of his father or the death of a friend or the death of a loved one was like a coronation. Those left behind inherit the duties of the departed, divide them up among themselves, and carry on the memory. When the news of his father's death arrived, he was in the garden of his friend the Judge, lying on a rug under the large orange tree with tea by his side. They had to wake him from a catnap. He told himself that the matter was over and done with, but he didn't know whether it was like a sigh of relief or like salvation. During that period, not a day went by without his thinking about it. When it finally happened, was he relieved from the burden of waiting?

Ishaq Effendi died in his rocking chair. Sleep and death took him simultaneously. He was wearing his bright robe and his round glasses. There was a pomegranate rind next to him that his daughter had tossed him to moisten his throat against the dryness he used to suffer from at night. Ishaq Effendi had reached eighty-seven years of age without changing very much. His appearance hadn't changed, and it even seemed that he became clearer, more complete with age. The older he got, the more he came to resemble himself: his eyes became sharper, his nose more solid, his expressions more compassionate, his voice louder. He didn't change, even when his occupation changed from Ottoman employee to religious fanatic. In his own home, he went on behaving like a little prince. He stayed that way until there wasn't a single servant left. Only then did his mood soften. He was no longer able to buy himself new suits. His daughter was forced to fix up his old ones to make them last, and she ended up with a scar that was as straight as a sword.

8 Abbas Beydoun

Ishaq Effendi hadn't worked a day in his life. During Ottoman times, he "worked" as a parks employee, which was really only a job in name; it was more like a nickname than an occupation. He didn't have the patience to manage his properties, so peasants squatted on them. When the French came and abolished his position, he went completely belly up. Only his suits and temperamental mood maintained his public standing. When it became clear that the effendi didn't really have anything else to do, he got really angry. He spoke in anger, explained things in anger, prayed in anger, and when religiosity finally swept him away, he came to resemble an angry prophet sporting a fez, spending his nights in prayer, making shrill appeals, as if judging God Himself for His patience and mercy.

My father never could have predicted that precisely eighty-seven years had been written for his father. In his dreams, he always saw himself in some sort of wasteland at his father's funeral, unable to be sad or to cry at the burial, with people staring at him, talking all around him, until they all got up and left him alone. When his father finally died, he was liberated from those dreams. He wasn't afraid until he arrived at the house. The others had arrived before him. No one seemed to care how he was feeling. They immediately gave him his father's chair, watch, and cloak, and waited for him to sit down, angry and silent as he always was. The atmosphere was dynamic as everyone busily arranged for the following day's funeral. They nearly forgot he was there, so he slipped away without anyone's noticing. He headed upstairs, where they had enshrouded his father. He found him fully covered, laid out on a table. He moved toward him and lifted the shroud from above his head. What hair was left had accumulated into dry, useless little clumps on his father's forehead, as though they had been formed from dried mud or glue, or constructed out of wires and felt. He saw his father's eyes arching toward the ceiling: frozen, thunderstruck, plastic. No vision or spark left in them. Just glass. Petrified glass.

Panic struck him; he felt nothing but fear. He had denied his father from the beginning. He stood still for a second, unable to find a single ounce of courage in his heart. He tried to regain his composure, to reclaim some courage, but he didn't have a foot to stand on. He was a coward. Here was the moment of truth; he would never be anything but a coward. All he wanted was to stop running away. But he would never return to that room. All he could see were the eyes of the dead turned to stone. His insides were dry and plastic like the gaze of that dead man as it was transformed into glass. He tried forcing himself to cry, but couldn't. There wasn't a single drop in his entire body. He continued trying until he realized the futility of his effort and stopped. But in that attempt he managed to shed his sadness, or at least that shroud he believed was sadness. Only discomfort remained: a self intolerant of itself. He was created without the ability to endure. He simply had to go back downstairs. All of the guests were moving about, making a commotion. They didn't notice his coming or going. A dead old man in a rocking chair: the most normal of things. He grew increasingly uncomfortable. His disinterest made him and his father even. Death was what they had always talked about, what they rose and fell over, what they came back to and repeated all the time. He felt the edges of the sofa squeezing his body more and more. All the old men fell asleep in their chairs. Two young men in the courtyard quarreled amicably. It was close to midnight, but he wasn't sleepy, and as time approached the zero hour, he couldn't hear or feel a thing. Every struggle ended. His senses, his soul, faded away, and he became perfectly still.

In the morning, he found them propping up his father's best friend as he cried in their arms. He envied that man for the tears streaming down his cheeks—bountiful, wet tears that sprang from pockmarked skin, taut as a piece of paper. Those falling tears preceded words; words collided with front teeth not fixed firmly into place. A ghastly scene: the sheikh staggered among outstretched arms, tears pouring out of his eyes like water from a leaky bladder. My father was embarrassed when they noticed he wasn't crying. Someone yelled, "God is great, his tears are burning!" This meant that sadness had incinerated his tears. His teary-eyed cousin sobbed from time to time. He detested him even more than usual. He heard the women sobbing nearby. He felt his body preparing for something, as if it were about to be crucified by a scream that hadn't come out yet. He was as solid as a pillar. It was as if he could actually feel his bones growing, his fingernails lengthening. An overwhelming anger suddenly came over him; he could easily have killed someone. But he went along with them on this path that they purposefully lengthened. They walked all the way around the cemetery to enter it from the other side.

Safia didn't say a word when I greeted her at the front door. Once more she extended to me her luscious palm and her long, full fingers. The strange thing was that, this time, my aunt was the one who greeted her with a welcome so exaggerated that it reached the point of hostility. The two sat down and reminisced about the immigrants' houses filled with lots of black servants, cooks, and drivers, holidays and afternoons, fond memories. They didn't mention once the man in whose memory they had been brought together.

I was the only man in the house. The deaths of my uncle, then my dad, and then my brother in Abdu's accident had made me a survivor. Sometimes I felt like my salvation had meaning. I was the only man for three generations, which granted me a painful distinction. I spent most of my time like someone recuperating from an illness, feeling as if the three deaths were somehow an interconnected series of events. I couldn't understand why, but I regularly spent long stretches of time at home flipping through books in which I was able to find traces of my father's reading. Those books didn't help me very much in getting to know my father and, like him, told me very little. Just some proper names, dates, and indexes, like those little notebooks he used to sit down with every night, scribbling words and numbers, the harvest of his day, in them. I didn't believe that this kind of life could be for anyone but him. I still imagine that he lived on dates and titles alone.

From my room, I could hear things without needing to decipher them, just like I always used to. I could hear my aunt's loud voice, typically in response to something else I couldn't hear. Safia and my aunt immediately drifted into these conversations. My mother, who had been uncomfortable from the start with my aunt's return to our house after my father's death, left the two of them alone. In shock, she told me that Safia was married and that her husband had come with her. I was surprised, too, but I quickly figured out that my mother perceived Safia's visits as a sign that something wasn't right with her marriage. When I asked Safia about it, the question didn't bother her. She told me that she had a daughter and that she would like to invite me over to her house sometime. The visit didn't take place until after I bumped into her on the street. She handed me one of her two shopping bags to carry and led me to the entrance. The sun was blistering. I noticed the color of her skin—coffee with milk—that seemed to fracture into an out-of-place whiteness. It was silky and radiant, and I could feel its fertility, how singular her color was. The first time I saw her, she was wan and autumnal. On that occasion, I managed to take a long look at her dense, coal black hair that she casually tossed aside and that, along with her short sleeves, made her look like a young man.

She swiftly clambered up the stairs on the balls of her feet. Sure of herself and independent, she didn't look a thing like the woman I had concocted based on my aunt's memories or the strange furniture she had brought with her.

In the deepest recesses of that room, in the spectral darkness beneath the dresser, the little girl was hiding out. I didn't notice her until she stirred, opening two brilliant, penetrating eyes. Her face, too, was the color of coffee with milk, but it was smaller, set between long, thick curls that made her whole body seem tiny. Her hair resembled her mother's. She only rarely scraped the dryness and bumps from her skin so that later in life she would have her mother's white complexion as well as her touch. Her fingers were round and interlaced, sloughing off their dryness to become like her mother's fingers. Safia didn't acknowledge her, unloading the bags in the kitchen while I got overheated sitting there, ensconced in one of her many large, classically upholstered couches with their engraved arms and decorated backs. Wine-colored splotches with large green flowers—such is the furniture we occasionally inherit from our ancestors and always seem to have piled high, impossible to arrange because there is never enough space for it and never any light that suits it. It is imprisoned in chambers that aren't prepared for it, looking terrible and shadowy no matter where it is put, its harshness and resistance seeming like an affront. I sat at the point I calculated was the middle and noticed that my feet didn't quite touch the ground, making the tear in my socks visible. When I became aware of that, I saw that the sock was twisted, but I wasn't sure how to fix it. When I pulled my foot out and started to pull the sock over my toes and then my heel, the little girl approached me and stood there to watch what I was doing. She looked less like her mother than I had thought at first; her face was rounder, her fingers stubbier, but she certainly had her mother's gaze: a penetrating look, with a wrinkle by her eye that nearly made me burst out laughing, a look that was usually the mark of genealogy and generations. She burst out laughing as she stared at me. The hole in my sock was apparently entertaining. I didn't have any trouble fixing it. She climbed onto one side of the tall couch; as a matter of fact, she sidled right up next to me. She got down on her knees and proceeded to touch my face and hair, but what really amused her was the depression in the back of my head against which she pressed her hand. She didn't look that much like her mother, after all, but with that gaze and that touch—especially that touch—she all but became her. These feelings puzzled me the whole time she was searching for protuberances and depressions on my head, until I started to become overly sensitive to her and could no longer abide her fingers on my face. I shook my head away in a sudden motion. Her expression morphed into panic. She drew away from me and hurriedly hopped off the couch, but didn't cry. She stood a short distance away, transfixed, and continued staring at me. Then a sound went up—a high, shrieking sound that got progressively higher, a clear screech without tears or a single clear utterance. Her mother wasn't concerned. All her daughter required was a gentle touch in order to calm down. Then she ran off, disappearing completely once again.

A collection of unframed paintings were hanging on the wall, their colors dense—red splattered like a fresh splotch of blood, screaming yellow—but the most important thing was the glossy overcoat that had been generously applied, making the paintings as shiny as mirrors. She said that her husband Hashim taught painting at the club. She sat down next to me on the couch and talked about my father, whom she used to see passing by her house on his way to school and returning home with a large, overstuffed bag, his cane guiding his way. She said that she found him incredibly handsome and respectable. She said she had heard a lot about me and didn't expect me to be any different from my father. There *were* differences: my curly hair, my narrow eyes, and other things about myself I didn't particularly care for. As if sensing my feelings, she looked at me with a charitable expression. I had never been happy with my appearance, and when my oval face started to grow longer during adolescence, I started to notice, as I nervously regarded myself in the mirror, how much it resembled a foot. My hair was what first turned on me. I hated its unkemptness and its coarseness. I felt as if it never truly got clean, that it rested atop my head like straw. In fact, my entire head was heavy and overgrown in an annoying way. Anyway, that's an old story. It all started when my mother said that I had a big mouth: "Hajjeh Raziyyeh Jowls," she used to call me. My younger brother reviled me with this nickname, "Hajjeh Raziyyeh Jowls," whenever I tried to pick a fight with him or whenever I insulted him about his weight.

My father kept trying to draw water from his eyes, but didn't succeed. Everyone who laid eyes on him cried, yet he could not. But no one made anyone cry the way they made that young man cry whom they didn't know anything about. My father couldn't recall if he had cried the day his mother died, when he was still just a little boy. No doubt he hadn't shed any tears before that moment. He was wounded because he had been a strange boy who passed into orphanhood with-out shedding any tears. He was gripped by a desire for her, for other times and people that had slipped from his mind. Still, it wasn't easy for him to remember his brother. The more he tried, the more he felt a new kind of discomfort, like moving mountains or giving sight to the blind, like not feeling anything. At one moment, he let his true feelings show. It wasn't easy for him to locate clear feel-ings or photos, as if memory suddenly fell ill, growing annoyed or even damaged as it became ever more isolated and subject to pressure. There wasn't a single incident from his childhood, most of which he had spent bickering, that he actu-ally remembered. As if nothing deserved to be remembered, as if he had gotten rid of his memories like one throws away so many old pairs of shoes, he didn't have any memories of his brother. And although they had spent their childhood quarreling with one another, he was always the one who had started the hitting. He would start for whatever reason—he thought his brother was too scrawny, or he didn't recognize his right to exist. He'd hit him as if he himself wasn't doing anything at all, as if he were hitting something he didn't actually see. Is that why his brother was erased from his memory? Is that why he always seemed so form-less? He preferred his brother to stay like that because he didn't ever want to be with him, didn't want for them both to enjoy the same right to exist, the same rank. He thought he couldn't remember a single incident, but then he managed to recover one that came to him in a mechanical sort of way: unable to respond, to speak, to have a voice, he had swung at his brother like someone fanning away a foul stench. He never expected his brother to fight back and, of course, was sur-prised when his brother finally did. As if the blow had been intended to decimate this thought about him, his brother's response came powerfully and constituted a rupture in every sense of the word. The fact that his brother was still around, that he was still right there in front of him, baffled him. So the boy that was my father did nothing but hit him, blindly raining blows down upon him, as though somehow reducing him to zero in this way.

His brother was very fat when he was younger, especially relative to his own extreme skinniness. Despite his mother's pride in his brother's vigor, in which she perceived her own strength, he was treated like little more than a run-of-the-mill glutton. They could have no aspirations for a boy like that. They conceded how difficult it was to find anything that captured his attention. Although he didn't disappoint their expectations, he did lag during his early school years, only to confront a legacy of his sibling's intelligence and superiority. My father had felt visceral distaste for his overweight brother ever since that boy's birth. As far as he was concerned, his brother was nothing more than a sack of meat, and he used to believe that his touch alone could be harmful. He was stunned to find that other mothers admired his brother's white color, health, and wide eyes, and that friends, his own personal friends, thought his brother was nice. He used to wish that his brother would remain an invisible sack of meat forever.

Later he realized that he hadn't known the first thing about his brother in those days. He never thought of him as someone worth knowing anything about. He didn't consider him worthy of having friendships or hobbies, of having a life at all. He used to be surprised to find out that his brother was loved, that he had any friends. He thought of him as nothing but a disgrace, a disgrace that could not be outrun, a disgrace without name, without description, without form, most certainly without an image.

His brother went with him to the intersection. They ventured away from their father, who had stopped to bargain with the merchant, and when he found his brother still next to him, he pushed him away. He didn't want to be with him, but the fat one wouldn't budge. He got angry at the fat one's following him, step after step, and when he noticed him pause to gape at a parrot in a cage, he ditched him. He walked under an archway, stopping to marvel at it and at the slaughtered animals hanging from metal hooks outside the entrance to the market, which was occupied predominantly by shoe sellers. There was nothing so pleasing as those hooks in that market, which looked more like the new building that had recently been added onto the market in town—brand new and clean. But the shops were nearly deserted because it was teatime, and all the merchants had congregated in one of the stalls to drink. He slipped away and found himself at a small intersection. The city he knew ended there; from there on, he would have to rely on instinct. Disoriented, he decided to make a right turn. He took one short step and then climbed some stairs. He saw a dome to the right and a market to the left. He retraced his steps without making sure if it was the way back or if he was continuing on in the wrong direction. He walked down an alley that quickly opened up. He felt lost. He stood still, seeing the street fan out before him and lead down to a large plaza. He came out of the alley to stand somewhere he was convinced had no name. He didn't cry, but heard the fat one crying nearby. They walked hand in hand as the fat one led him back to the turnoff, the intersection, the bridge, and finally dragged him back to where they had first been separated from their father. The merchant coaxed them into staying with him until their father returned. The fat one wasn't stupid, then, and this wasn't the only incident to show it. One time, when he couldn't get his older sister's sewing machine to work, he patiently removed a screw, but something suddenly fell from above him. He held it in his hand before it fell down and disappeared on the ground along with the screw. He pressed down hard on the pedal until the needle broke. He didn't dare make any more sudden movements. He drew away from the machine and stood up, unable to move until he saw his brother pick up the screw and the cover, stand on a small chair, and resecure them.

He used to push his brother away whenever he was next to him, and then he would draw away, so he couldn't understand how it was that whenever he needed something, his brother would appear, holding it. He remembered flopping around in those baggy clothes that his sister picked up for him dirt cheap in the market. They were used, probably a dead man's personal effects; she claimed not to know where they had come from and forced him to wear them. He remembered that jacket with those bulging pockets and gold buttons that was too short for his brother and that he wore with something like happiness. They didn't do that for his brother, who never had to wear clothes that were too big on him. He remembered making a tall fat man with short legs out of wood he had collected on the beach. It was the beginning of the electrical era, and his brother understood everything with an electrician's intuition, repairing his older sister's sewing machine on a number of occasions. But she still smuggled food to the older brother. He remembered how his brother was his father's toy, how his father squeezed those whitish, bloated cheeks, how his sister played with him—in effect, how his brother was the entire neighborhood's plaything. Everyone was attracted to his vigor and his whiteness, but, of course, nothing compared to the older brother's presentation of his high marks. Of course, nothing compared to the eloquent expressions that came out of his mouth. Rather, nothing compared to his profound yet unintentional aptitude that was evidence of a deep understanding.

There were always lots of people in Safia's house. Hashim's flashy paintings were on display everywhere. Though they seemed powerful at first glance, it became obvious that it was a power without substance. He claimed to know me through my father, the intellectual of the city. I was the least acquainted with that intellectual culture.

16 Abbas Beydoun

All I can remember is the high, mellifluous tone of his voice, which didn't leave enough space for me to differentiate between his words. Hashim was all smiles. Then there were his stare and the perfectly dull blue into which he welcomed his guests. Blond curls were spontaneously held in place against his forehead, and soft lines crisscrossed his face. His was a hospitable face with no place for exhaustion or rigidity. Hashim's beauty was light, easy evanescence, a ruse of simplicity. We rarely wanted to put our confidence in him without thinking it over first. I noticed him getting closer than I would have liked. He praised my father profusely and didn't allow me to finish muttering the humble expressions I tried to respond with. I didn't care much for this sort of talk about my father because it was little more than the sign of someone who had made his acquaintance but didn't actually known anything about him: "brain . . . mind . . . magnificence" . . . blah blah blah. I calmly listened to Hashim, staring vacantly at his face, which was colored in a way that was quite different than his paintings. I was terrible at giving compliments. I rarely knew how to articulate them without getting tongue-tied.

On one occasion, I found myself alone on the couch with Safia. Once again I felt her fingers brush against my hand as Hashim rambled on like a newscaster, speaking in the jargon-laden vernacular of news reports. His was the accent of the "immigrants" who spoke formal radio Arabic and tried to mimic a kind of imprecise eloquence. He spoke like an uneducated man parroting superficial knowledge. I didn't appreciate this about him. That dialect ruined his reputation in a way I couldn't ignore. Whenever my senses are offended by some such dissonance, it tends to put me in a bad mood. I walked away from him while he was still talking—almost without hearing a thing, as though I were protecting my ears from an annoying interruption. In any event, that talking didn't last very long. He apparently had vomited everything he had to say. In the meanwhile, the little girl, who had just disappeared, came back to sit in her father's room. I tried playing with her but backed away when she indicated to me her readiness to let out another scream. Hashim showed me his paintings. From the other room, he brought more paintings that consistently reinforced my negative impression. Viewing his work was interesting enough at first, but quickly devolved into an excruciating bore. I didn't say anything, nor did he expect me to. He shouted at the girl, who was attracted to the red of one painting but didn't know how to appreciate it properly. The girl was consumed by a long scream and ran off, disappearing once again.

In Hashim's living room, there were often students from classes that had just let out. For some reason, they all seemed to have well-known fathers: election bosses, noted bank employees, entrepreneurial businessmen. He also used to host young party leaders and army officers. His visitors got acquainted with one another without trying too hard to gain each other's trust and, for the most part, without paying much notice when they happened to run into each other elsewhere. Inside the house, they did whatever they felt like—making phone calls, even from the bedrooms, closing the door behind them without being sure to lock it; going to the bathroom for a quick shower or to the kitchen to make a sandwich. Just imagine. I might see a coffee drinker beside a beer drinker or someone else holding a glass of soda. There were lots of them, and they weren't very interested in each other; perhaps they weren't even interested in Hashim either. But there was one person they always turned to greet whenever she came around, to exchange a few words or a cheerful look with her whenever they passed by her, one single woman: Safia.

Hashim dedicated a painting I despised to me—a slave drawn in blood red, trudging forward despite the chains binding his feet, with a contorted body and a raised arm ending in a clenched fist, like a statue made entirely from muscle. Hashim called it *The Awakening,* but all I could think of was hemorrhaging, rape, a penis, something like prehistoric animals erupting out of a momentary lapse in imagination and intelligence. Out of all the stories Hashim told us about his life, he never once explained how it was that he ended up an artist. He talked about wide spaces in the jungle, on the banks of a rushing river, fenced in and flanked with guards, where dozens of people worked night and day under powerful lights in search of diamonds. He showed me a picture of himself there wearing golf pants and a straw hat. They found the giant diamond, larger than any other. They didn't find a buyer right away, so they placed it in the bank for safekeeping. One night a group of Africans surrounded the bank, burned it to the ground, and the diamond disappeared. Hashim says that they were his rivals, but that the company had organized the whole thing.

Safia was uninterested. It was obvious that she had heard him spin this yarn on more than one occasion. She dragged the girl from her secret hiding place in the closet and sat her down in her room to brush her hair. Whatever he left out of the story, Safia filled in later. He had moved off the estate, entrusting it to his partner, who said that it was a losing venture and that the best thing to do would be to abandon it. Hashim was unsuccessful, didn't listen, and didn't really care, so he gave up the business for a cheap price. "His partner was rich, and us, well, as you can see," Safia said. Hashim flashed a smile that seemed unconnected to its meaning. Safia got annoyed at how difficult it became to annoy him. Whenever he started talking about his connections with the political bosses, she would bark at him, "That's enough!" and he would shut up. My aunt said she was certain that his father always arranged an unknown young man for him until he grew tired of him. But Musa confessed that Hashim had been the one to orchestrate the bank fire, so the jig was up. They threw him in jail for one year, until his father was able to use his connections to get him released. But the diamond had vanished without a trace. Musa said that the whole thing might be nothing more than one of Hashim's tall tales. What Musa didn't say was how Hashim went on to become an informer for the diamond prospectors, how he conspired with them to murder and ended up getting wounded in the leg. After he recovered, his father sent him to Lebanon. They say that he never cozied up to the officers for any reason, but many people still didn't trust him one bit.

After his mother died, my father thought of himself as an orphan. He was as skinny as a rail. The more his sisters saw him like that, the more they cried. As if his weakness alone was proof of their mother's absence. Someone of his weight, though, could hang from any branch and climb any wall. Just by placing his foot on a rock, he felt as if he were falling upwards. A sensation like flight helped spirit him up into a tree to seek refuge in its branches. A sensation like flight allowed him to walk as though he were hovering above the earth. When he fell, he returned safely down to the ground, like an airplane. He fell from the roof above the kitchen and the heights of the China tree without feeling the impact of hitting the ground, without getting hurt. In every moment of such a fall, he felt as if he were truly flying, later trying to remember how he had done it, but unable to do so.

No one paid any attention to his fat brother's orphanhood. He was content with food as his company, so they left him alone and didn't really notice how after his mother's death he started growing even fatter; he kept expanding until he nearly exploded. As he gained weight, his face became rounder, the skin under his chin sagged, and his dimples shimmered. But his attractiveness also increased somehow, and everyone was drawn to hugging and kissing him. His two sisters braided his hair, put necklaces around his neck and bracelets around his wrists. He ate as much as he possibly could, unconsciously eating just about anything; they would always find the bowls empty and the kneading machine without dough. He always seemed to find his way to the food his two sisters creatively tried to hide for the older brother. In the end, it seemed as though a small predator or a thief were living in their house. He moved less and less and started finding it difficult to keep up with the other children's games, but he stayed with them, sitting on the stone bench, just sleeping mainly, as flies buzzed around his lips and eyes. The children had to struggle just to wake him up. They tickled him on his sides until he woke up laughing, pushing them away as he laughed, then turning on them with his massive body. They would run off, screaming. He went back into the house every once in a while, then returning with something to eat in his hand; he never refused to share with anyone who asked him for a bite. Whenever he woke up in the middle of the night wracked with hunger pangs, he dashed off to the pantry and ate the first thing he could gets his hands on—plain bread or rice. But he wasn't one to complain when he didn't find anything to eat. He would lie in bed awake, alert. An hour might go by. Whenever someone passed by for some reason or another, he would watch with calm eyes, slowly robbing them of their comfort.

He was mellow and rarely cried over anything. Were those calm, gentle eyes recording something . . . recording how the others worshiped his older brother and served him by stashing food for him and setting him apart with clothes, listening to every word he said with pride, without forcing him to do anything he didn't feel like doing? Was this why he was so much like an eating machine, uninterested in studying or talking, always desperately trying to get his hands on some food in whatever way possible, consumed with stuffing his face in order to stave off the possibility of having to talk or move or do anything else?

He went on like that after his mother's death—twelve years neglected, using his massive body as a wedge against every hope inside him. They would have thought him incapable of any expression at all if they hadn't seen some knowing glances. They marveled at his ability to learn trades—that is to say, at his astonishing ability. When electricity came to the town, there was only one technician that the company ever sent to do repairs, and the boy did nothing but observe that man working until after a while he was able to repair a line himself. That ability became a real burden for him. The neighbors started calling him at every little breakdown, and even as the requests piled up, he continued to respond without fail. This certainly made him into a source of wonderment for the entire neighborhood as they started to prefer him to his washed-up, absent-minded brother. When he fixed a radio, his father congratulated him; they talked him up in front of everybody. His father, who had never worked an honest day in his life, recognized his son's skill, though, and congratulated him. He had always denigrated the satisfaction that comes from a job well done, which was the sign of a mind at ease and merited no respect as far as he was concerned.

Was my father's skinniness really proof of his orphanhood? When he learned that his terminally ill mother was dead forever, he immediately realized that he had become an orphan, but he wasn't shocked. The word intrigued him, and for some reason he couldn't understand, he felt that it was a badge of distinction. She had been ill for six years, precisely his brother's age, and he never complained about the fact that she was going to die, even when the moment finally arrived. After it happened, he didn't have to wait any longer. He wasn't relieved, but at least he wasn't waiting anymore. He was able to stand for a little while longer, to fill his lungs with air. Anyway, that wasn't what truly concerned him. Since her death, he had been nervous about completely forgetting what his mother looked like. Not only what she had looked like, but her name, her presence—all of it becoming as if she had never existed at all. From that first moment, death took her absolutely. He felt as if her absence had become a gaping hole within himself, something he couldn't deny: a chasm filled with nothingness. He heard many voices and opened his mouth to begin ridding himself of them. He sensed the futility of this act, but the ease with which those robust, powerful voices came out intrigued him still further. The more he released them, the clearer and more plaintive they became, and the greater his pleasure in them, too. Ayyy . . . Ayyy . . . that was from him—voices. Everything stopped when the others heard him. Everyone fell silent. He was with his maternal aunts in that spacious room, and they all fell completely silent, staring at him in spite of themselves. The oldest one let her hand that he had just shaken fall, and the second one made certain of the connection and stopped dancing. There was no longer anything but his own voice, cracking the ceiling and bouncing off the walls, coming and going. He tossed it up like he was flying a kite. He threw it, secured it, and brought it back. He was still full with it when he became extremely tired and fell silent. Afterward, though, he felt as though he had been emptied of everything, even his own voice. He laid his head down in his aunt's room and slept, leaving the entire funeral gathering confused. He needed time to rejuvenate, to return to his natural state. Many years later, after news of his brother reached him, he felt the renewed fear of never finding a picture of him within himself, of discovering that he didn't have anything left inside, at the heart of things. He felt this renewed, dreadful weakness in his emotions, that there was no truth in such feelings, that it was possible to forge or fabricate them. He was ashamed of doing that, of bringing it back, so he sat with everyone, silent and angry with himself. They were always around him, and he felt that he would remain in this condition as long as they were around him. He never had a moment to himself, so he pulled himself together, dropped everything, and went to Tyre.

Was my uncle's fatness really a by-product of his happiness? No one spoke of how they had to pull him off my dead mother's chest or how, whenever they came home, they would find him clinging to her bosom once again. After she was buried, they awoke and were unable to find him, so they went looking for him throughout the neighborhood. After they found him out wandering and brought him back home, he didn't say a word, nor did it cross anyone's mind that he might have gotten lost on the way to her grave. They didn't understand why he started speaking with a lisp and a stutter again. They thought he deserved it. They weren't surprised to find him trying on his mother's clothes, which they considered a sign of his terrible malaise or an unforgivable transgression. Nobody considered that he might have been just smelling the clothes. Just smelling them. Instead, they hurriedly threw them out of the house. He spent days walking around in search of them without asking or speaking. They thought that nothing could threaten their happiness, and he didn't behave in such a way to make them think otherwise. He was a slave to the family, to the neighborhood, a comrade of the other kids and the animals, restrained in his violence and his fighting, submissive to a fault. Only his family ever speculated that this attitude was a result of his lethargy, his ennui, and they were stunned to find him sinking his fingernails into his brother's face, the brother who had kicked him for no other reason than that he had found him in this condition. The brother who used to do that whenever he saw him, to avoid tripping over this apathetic sack, to force him, with his arms or his legs or whatever it took, out of his way.

He went on eating whatever he could get his hands on. He threw it down his gullet until he was sated. His bowels were filled with strength and determination.

Tranquility didn't last long, though, as fullness constantly tried to overpower emptiness. When emptiness got the upper hand again, he was alone for a moment as his strength melted, his defenses were slowly ground down, and he got hungry again. He had to fight off that emptiness. It wouldn't allow him a moment's rest. He had to keep his hand in his mouth, to refuel himself continuously.

When his two sisters saw him in that condition, they prepared whatever would best keep his stomach full. Pots filled with potatoes or beets or creamed wheat were placed in front of him, and he tucked right into all of it. He devoured whatever he could find, without discriminating, chewing slowly to keep himself alive or more balanced. He swallowed those disgusting morsels one bite after another, until food lost its taste and there was nothing left but that frightening need to swallow. Potatoes acquired a terrible tastelessness, like pulped paper and things that have been overchewed. It was the taste of fear itself.

I forgot about my uncle after everything that happened. For a long time, my father had imprisoned us in his brother's story, until, when we grew up, we escaped it. My father died, and it seemed as though the story had never actually been real in the first place. A story without a key: all we knew was the ending, an ending that was like an unused ticket past its expiration date, an obituary for a name that received no eulogy. Safia didn't talk about my uncle at all, and no one pressured her to. My mother was the only one who ever tried, but she was quickly confronted by two silences—her own and that of my aunt, who clearly had no idea what to do, so she simply clammed up. I found myself identifying with that silence for no reason. Maybe I had inherited that instinct to behave as she behaved and, as I supposed in secret, as my dad also used to behave simply by virtue of being a member of this family. My mother's questions seemed to be nothing more than idle curiosity coming from outside the family.

The mourning held in our house for my uncle was solemn. In our house, his name had been mentioned with trepidation and furtive glances toward my father. So my mother, who had rashly turned away in silence, seemed eager to know the details of my uncle and Safia's relationship. When she asked Safia if she was one of my uncle's women, Safia's eyes suddenly dilated and then returned to their normal size once again. I carefully guarded Safia's secret from my mother. Safia rarely talked about my uncle, but I was interested to hear about him from her.

He had been just a name to me, besieged and encircled inside me, and there was nothing left of him after my father's passing.

As soon as news of my uncle arrived, my mother reached out her hand and took down the only picture of him that was still hanging on the wall in my grandfather's house, the one that had remained in our possession for a long time. I didn't see that picture again until I found it twenty years later in a metal box. Although I had hoped to find more like it, I was disappointed. We had no other mementoes of my uncle, so my mother's efforts to cast out his name and forbid it in our house ceased. As far as she was concerned, and as far as we were concerned, that was the greatest honor that a memorial could provide: to rise above the energy of remembrance and language. That was her way of mourning—it was my father's way and it was our way later on. It was obvious that my father couldn't bear the memory of his brother, so we all collaborated to keep him from it. It was preferable for us not to mention him at the table so the soup wouldn't stop in our throats, so we wouldn't break down under the weight of his memory. It was preferable for us to attend his memorial without his memory scorching us. Our mourning was a complete absence that we often suspected ran parallel to our own lives. Complete absence: not even half of an ordinary day devoted to the dead before they are finally laid to rest. My mother's all-consuming void rounded out that imaginary emptiness in which we all lived. As a sign of great fear and abiding loyalty, the Yazidis cast the devil out of their speech—not just his proper name, but every name and every utterance that approximates it—and that's just what we did. The name "Musa" was no longer uttered, even though it was quite common in our family, and there was scarcely a household that didn't have one of its own. Relatives didn't visit without a big Musa or a little Musa, nudging him toward my father with pride, pride in the belief that this one deserved that name, graciously emulating my uncle, mainly by inventing stories about him.

My mother had plenty of ways to make people understand not to burden my sick father with their stories. They'd immediately fall silent, ashamed that they had even come. After that, it became customary to lock up the children bearing that name somewhere else in the house before visiting my father and to avoid mentioning my uncle's name or talking about him, despite the fact that most of them found this injunction to be blasphemous—religion commands us to endure tragedy. Some of them feared what the outcome of this conceited-ness would be for us and, of course, hated my mother for it. Their visits to us dwindled. My mother believed that this was the best way to protect my father. She thought that by closing the door and banishing the name, she might be saved from it, as though her sadness was an infection from outside.

As far as she was concerned, sickness, fear, corruption, and even death were viruses outside the house, and as long as we stayed in our rooms, we wouldn't be exposed to them. She always wanted us to stay inside the house. She caressed my hair and my brother's, vowing to keep us by her side until we were at least ten years old. Even inside the house, she preferred that we played near her. When out of desperation my sister left her room for the first time after seven years of waiting, she was afraid of the huge, full-grown tree in the corner of the neighborhood and started pointing at it with her finger, screaming and crying.

My mother was the neighborhood healer and perhaps its oracle, too; for every illness, she had a remedy. She read fortunes not only in coffee cups, but also in seashells and playing cards. With her flowing hair, flared nostrils, and floppy ears, she commanded respect and struck terror in the hearts of others, but she was unable to allay their fears, even with all of those spells and amulets that she didn't much believe in anyhow. She pronounced those spells, laughing at herself and laughing even more when she saw how impotent she actually was. We'd find those amulets neglectfully cast aside all around the house, fraying at the edge, with visible writing on them. She prayed at her leisure and didn't believe in anyone or anything, not even her god. She relied on her strength alone, and this frightened her even more. She behaved like an oracle who didn't believe in her own powers or even in the unknown itself anymore. When my father was drowning in his depression, she was the only one who didn't advise him to be treated with magic. Of course, she didn't cast a single spell of her own upon him; I don't remember her throwing an amulet around any of our necks, either. She never stopped worrying about us or about herself, although maybe that was because she knew better than anyone that nothing could truly protect any of us. And for some reason she was always fighting against weakness, as if she were prepared for any danger—not the danger of illness and death alone, but the danger of poisoning, drowning, falling; the danger of poverty and abandonment.

When my aunt returned from Africa, she waited barely two days before telling me that my other aunt was going to marry my father. When her own mother had died, she had subjected her father the sheikh to every suspicion. She had accused her "holy father," as everyone used to call him, of sleeping with her maternal aunt and the servant's wife. She hadn't trusted him or herself. Deep down inside, she compared herself to other people, finding nothing but selfishness and doubt. She didn't find anything within herself that would allow her to believe in other people. She maneuvered, deceived, and disappeared. The drama of weakness, illness, and now mourning. She kept people away from my dad and told them not to utter a word about his brother. The drama of mourning required that the dead not participate in anything. She was refusing to include her children in anything: didn't cook their favorite foods, didn't sit where they wanted her to, didn't look after their things or their clothes when they were out. After I disappeared completely into a boarding school, she stopped going into my room and forbade from the house all the foods and other things I liked. She always said she couldn't handle seeing the friends I hung out with or the homes I used to frequent.

But my father's silence was not as my mother would have wanted it to be. It was first and foremost his own father's custom or, rather, the family's custom during that time. They perceived remorse and grief as attributes of the rabble— weak and inappropriate. One day his father saw his only brother, who later was killed by someone from the Ayyub family, receiving all kinds of people: hugging some, shaking hands with others, and walking to greet still others—friendly with everyone. He perceived him to be intending to flatter those people, as a host will do for his guests. So what my mother didn't realize was that my dad talked about his brother with consideration and even a smile, as if someone had struck up a conversation about him. He was always waiting for a way in to that conversation through somebody else, but everyone was under my mother's watchful eye, which made it quite difficult. What my mother didn't know was that my father felt as if mourning suited her. She even looked pretty in her black outfit. He noticed how she didn't slow down after hearing the news. She ran around, kicking up dust from straw mats as he threw down blankets and she gathered up chairs in the middle of the house before letting out her first scream. She was awesome, even talented, at this, as though it were her profession. Her face seemed brilliant and youthful, gentle even. She was invigorated in her black clothes; it was her springtime. How mourning suited her, how strong and victorious it made her: death was her own private strength. He thought that she directed toward the dead the camaraderie she felt for him. In the end, he pulled himself together and left for Tyre.

What my mother didn't know was that my father could no longer tolerate her odor. The tears that he interminably tried to produce caused all those around him to cry, caused them to lose control over themselves. He wanted this same ability so badly that his skin tone receded inward, retreating like urine that isn't evacuated from the body, but in the end gets transformed, like all secretions, into an awful stench. His body secreted that odious stink, like putrid tears. My mother didn't have a very good sense of smell. Naturally, she couldn't smell herself or her husband or her children. The others, amazingly, couldn't smell anything either. Nevertheless, the smell remained in my father's nose until it really did start to seem like the smell of urine. She was rejuvenated after her bath, and my father sensed that it wasn't only tears, but besieged speech as well, and that if he spoke, if speech were possible, he would be liberated somewhat from the stench.

As usual, my father went first to the Judge's house, where the Judge welcomed him, cinching his belt around his bloated stomach. He was unable to close the robe completely so that at all times it exposed two bruised knees and his thick salt-and-pepper chest hair. His red hair matched the red of his eyebrows; this, the tip of his nose, and the corners of his eyes gave him the appearance of having been mass-produced. The Judge guided my father to the table, which was immediately set with dishes; he was presented with one plate after another. The Judge so much wanted him to be sated that he seemed prepared to feed him by hand if necessary. He said it wasn't purely coincidental that sorrowful occasions were also feasts. The heart also needs to eat, and there is nothing like food that allows us to satisfy the need for rejuvenation that beleaguers us when we lose somebody. He was talking about everything all at once, speaking in a raucous voice, chewing audibly, as if he needed to crush all his thoughts and words beneath his molars.

My father always knew that Loverboy would be the first to arrive. At first blush, Loverboy, as the Judge used to call him, seemed somehow larger than his delicate face, curly hair, and timid voice. But the young man who had duped the Judge into giving him a job at the court was truly seductive. Women—divorcées, women who had been denied their inheritances, women repudiated by their husbands—instinctively turned toward him without his lifting a finger. They all pursued him. He turned his eyes and head away from them without realizing that his way of sitting—like an orphan or a student in trouble—and his way of averting his eyes or nervously playing with his watch were actually turn-ons. Women approached him with a calmness that they felt in the depths of their bodies, typically needing to get even closer to him, to touch him. He hardly noticed the willingness with which they let down their guard with him or how it was that they would go home with him unafraid and leave without feeling any guilt. He would try in earnest to send them back to their houses, back to their men, but he usually ended up going out with whoever would best satisfy his desires. He would escort them to his widowed sister's house. He wasn't capable of behaving so casually with men, men who found his mystique repugnant and insufferable, and so treated him at times with neglect and condescension.

Loverboy didn't say anything at first. He stood there—his shirt flapping behind him like a sail, my father's shoulder against his arm—before sitting down, then repeating to himself how beautiful he had been, as though he alone bore the burden of being beautiful.

The Poet finally arrived. He was the oldest of the three, but no one knew his actual age, which he cagily kept hidden. The Judge had inherited this acquaintance from his father, and though the Judge had always made fun of him, the tall Poet, with his full shock of white hair, was actually quite handsome. News of his exploits with women and his economy were legend, as was his poetry, which he organized daily and kept on scraps of paper in his pocket, from which he read to them whenever they got together. They always lavished him with disingenuous praise.

The Poet didn't say a word to my father. His crying overwhelmed him, and he sobbed on my father's shoulder, who was still at a loss. As soon as he sat down, he said he had composed an elegy. Conversation among the three of them came to a halt, and they let him take it out of his pocket and read. It didn't really sound like a mourning poem. It was about a peeled orange rind. The Judge and Loverboy knocked it, but my father found it truthful. It really was that peeled orange—the pain he was feeling was nothing if not that. Simply a peeled orange, of any variety, that makes you feel nothing but nakedness and exposure. He thought how the death of his brother was like a kind of bareness. He felt as though they had cut off his right hand and that there was a hole in his heart that everyone could see.

The smell. It tickled his nose. It halted his breaths. His inhalation. The smell of old fish or withering flowers that only he could smell and not despair from. It was the smell of himself. It was coming not only from his skin, but from his heart, too. It wasn't just his burning tears, but his decrepit ideas. It wasn't just a smell. It could be an idea burrowing through his thoughts like a moth. It could be a whisper that disappeared, leaving a scent in its place. What if, he thought, the rankness wasn't a smell, but a kind of terror? Fat, sweat, urine: Isn't that what our insides are, first and foremost? How can the inhabitant of an odor no longer have a body to resist it? Nausea—yes, nausea—is the malady of those who cannot smell or, more likely, of those who aren't able to eliminate a smell in order to breathe clear. What suffering do they endure with such vague, weird, powerful smells that never return and that nothing can eliminate? What suffering comes with smells that are liable to vanish at a moment's notice or to get modified (Are they really smells?), transmogrifying into whispering and terror? My father thought of his aunt, who stared at her plate in terror, eating and drinking and living in disgust. Of course, all she had to do was tear into her skin to reach the secret of that wicked, metamorphosing smell. What suffering accompanies the body that in the end emits such noticeable secretions and odors? Where is the pure, untainted smell in this world? The smell with no core, the smell that is unable to change? The Smell—everysmell—originated in his body, which he saw like a carrier of insects and poisons. He longed to trap it there. He gently scratched his skin in search of it, to ensure that it wouldn't leave his body. He wanted it to remain trapped inside him. In the end, he found it, like a whisper, overwhelming him with fear as a vague ringing in his ears engulfed him. It became acrid, burning, until he had to escape to the bathroom, where he thought, like Lady Macbeth, that not even all the water in the world could possibly expunge that smell.

My father stayed at the Judge's house and avoided coming back to town. Day after day we waited for him, and time went by without any news from him. In the end, Loverboy showed up in his car. We piled all of our stuff in, and he drove us to Tyre.

The gluttonous fatty, a barrel of flesh, grew lengthwise out of his heaviness and filled out two powerful shoulders. Meanwhile, my father remained, in his own eyes, nothing more than a feeble dwarf. The fatty's body became a rock hard lump, and his bloated face was transformed into a skinny one with sunken features—overhanging eyebrows, shimmering droopy eyes, a square chin. My father lost his beauty. His face lengthened until it became as flat as a foot. He painfully started to notice that his hair was coarse, painful to run his fingers through, like something not part of his body, like wire or straw. The weird thing was that he had started to gain weight. He didn't get obese or anything, but the combination of his thickness and his short stature certainly made him look pudgy. In short, my dad loathed his body. He didn't accept that it was the body he was destined to have, as if it had somehow tricked him, stood in for his real body like an impostor. This couldn't be his height or his head. He hated his stunted legs and his crooked fingers. Perhaps what kept him up at night was the feeling that his upper half didn't fit with his lower half. His shoulders were broader than his torso, and his head didn't match his chest. He thought of his body as an amalgam of independent parts; it was difficult for him to see it as an integrated whole. He didn't believe his eyes, maybe because he spent so much time staring into the mirror, dumbfounded at what he saw. In the end, he grew tired of his body and neglected it completely, simply not caring about what he wore or whom he emulated, as if he were living a stranger's life. He didn't own this body and didn't quite know how to behave in it. He preferred having food in his hands to swimming; he preferred walking to running. He could do nothing more with his body without training it for something that it simply wasn't created for. He continued to feel alienated from it except when he made a mistake, when he stumbled, when a morsel fell out of his mouth, or when he dropped a glass without noticing, which burdened him with something that felt like a great sin or even a wound. Otherwise, he would forget all about it, feeling like others had no desire even to look at him.

His brother really stood out, and with little effort on his part. He looked good no matter how he was dressed and with no more than two flicks of a comb. He learned how to swim like a pro in just two days; he rode a bike on the first try. He was capable of doing anything simply by watching someone else do it. He became a barber by observing the barber; he became a tailor in a week, a carpenter on pure instinct. He was a genie of labor, a miracle of craftsmanship.

Loverboy told my father that a virile man was known by the power of his scent. He didn't care for Loverboy's insinuation. He was terrified when the doctor told him that the cause of his condition couldn't be detected inside his body and added—in the same monotonous voice that indicated a considerable burden weighing upon his words—that my father needed to take better care of himself. My father understood that he could no longer count on anyone's help. He was alone, as if he were being sacrificed to a starved lion. He heard the doctor go on to say that medicine couldn't do anything for him and that he was going to have to deal with this condition on his own. The doctor nearly groaned beneath the weight of what he had to say as it pressed down on his shoulders, his voice, his eyes. With the same effort, he added that he personally believed every human being must create something. This was all very hard on the doctor. My father didn't respond. The whole thing seemed simple enough, but he felt as though the doctor had rendered him impotent. Once he was back out in the street, he didn't think about anything in particular, but realized he had been stripped of any backbone he once had. He was alone, holding onto his very breath, and nothing could stop him from falling apart. A small thought would be enough to destroy him. He didn't believe there was anything inside himself capable of protecting him. Creativity meant nothing more to him than always being ready for a fight. This task was Sisyphean, one that he didn't have the strength for. It was as if he could rely only on life's randomness with him, on a kind of preternatural game, or on his own randomness with life. When that ended, he would surely fall apart.

But he didn't fall apart. He didn't shatter like glass. The stench prevented him from fading away. That awful smell kept him from wasting away into nothing. The doctor told him that medicine couldn't do anything for someone in his condition. He read somewhere how some Sufis exposed themselves to a smell like this whenever they experienced desire; they secluded themselves with it in order to become physically and spiritually renewed. The doctor was nothing more than a sick, middle-aged man. My father knew that the doctor's illnesses wouldn't faze him. Short and with a huge head, he kept on talking as he lazily walked around, filling the room with cigarette smoke as if, unconcerned by his smoke rings, he were rising above his disease, submitting to his fate.

My father didn't speak to the Judge about his situation because he had always felt that the Judge's mercy toward people was the fastest way to scare them off. Even if the Judge occasionally rose above his inherited aristocratic arrogance, he couldn't suppress his visceral distaste for long. If someone dirty was near him, he walked away; he couldn't bear to be around it. Still, my father's regular visits to the public bath amazed the Judge, who found it to be cause for great amusement.

"Take me to the cinema," Safia said in front of Hashim, who smiled knowingly. Since Safia had first contacted me, I had become a favorite in her and Hashim's house. I don't remember how her arm got intertwined with my hand or how she appeared with me in front of everyone like that, but I didn't once protest becoming her bosom buddy, her ever-present companion for picnics on the beach. We walked along the waves, and she threw her weight down upon me, the foam frothing between her feet. She wasn't too embarrassed to ask me to clasp my hands behind her neck, to massage it, to run my fingers through her hair with a deliberate slowness that soothed her headache. Maybe she purposefully sat on the couch touching me, letting her hair down as her breath rose and fell near my face. She usually tried to gauge my opinion of her clothes or her hairstyle when lots of people were around, and her mountains of little trespasses depended on my opinion. Wherever Safia put me, the others put me and without doubting that it was the place for me. Hashim in particular mimicked everything she did, surpassing her in his zeal. Whenever he saw her demand something of me, he smiled at me knowingly, pityingly. He was kind enough to take out the painting he was dedicating to me and then leave so I could look at it without having to offer an opinion. I used to be able to deal with Safia, to keep up with her even if it was only with some difficulty. I couldn't pull myself together or get into my own rhythm, but she didn't seem to mind. With a lift of her eyebrows, she could put me in my place.

As soon as the lights went down, the movie screen welcomed her face. I had to act like Safia by collecting all the fragments of myself from the fever of expectations, the sleepless night of waiting, the nightmarish worries, and to watch alongside her: that woman arriving from outside the group; a horse; her hand up to her neck; on her, around her, as she rode that horse to the spring. I surrendered to the vibrant, radiant blue on screen, but my attention was always fixed on that meaningful silence in the seat next to me. My chair felt constricting and uncomfortable. I almost felt like a captive. I didn't have the guts to make a move yet. I was a prisoner of the darkness and of the screen. Through all that waiting, time passed at an excruciatingly slow pace, flowing by cheaply, wasted. Safia was entranced watching the film, as if she had forgotten about me altogether. Whenever I noticed her out of the corner of my eye, I felt that she was trying to distance herself from me. The Cossack on screen arranged a rendezvous with the woman, and they met in front of the horse. Safia sat in rapt attention. I noticed the ushers' flashlights, comments from the audience, the commotion of those coming and going, violating the theater and the mood with every moment, making it impossible to find air or space. The moment passed. Everything was on display only to be mocked. It was impossible to trust the seemingly naked darkness. The woman unknotted her braids in the tent before the man standing in front of her and took off her white shirt. I placed my hand on the armrest, brushed it against her elbow, and deliberately left it there for a little while, but her arm didn't budge. She remained transfixed by the woman in her white underwear. Her eyes were wide open as the woman got into bed in her underwear to wait for the man who was still standing next to the tent. I relaxed a bit to enjoy the film, but whenever I stole a glance at her face, I saw that she was hopelessly engrossed in watching. A commotion in the theater; a flashlight beam across the front rows; someone leaving, letting out a grumbly voice. I suddenly had to go to the bathroom, a need that rapidly grew and became painful, but I couldn't move. Her elbow was still touching my arm, preventing me from moving it. This contact faded and became part of Safia's silence. Moans could be heard outside the tent, and the horse lifted its head. Music swelled louder than my eardrums could tolerate. All of a sudden, she turned toward me, brought her head in close, and I felt her hair on my cheek and repeated breaths on my face before she blurted in my ear, "What's wrong, don't you like the film?" I didn't reply, and she quickly went back to watching it. As morning dawned on the woman and man in bed, the chirping of birds were heard off-camera, and I felt her fingers clutch my hand, taking my fingers one by one and gently rubbing them before grabbing my palm. She returned to the film once again, but continued squeezing my hand.

Everything changed between my father and my uncle. My uncle was the only one who didn't fear electricity—dispatching it, summoning it, directing it wherever he pleased—the only one who played with the radio, dumping out its internal parts and then putting them back together. The last one to be deterred by the clock's flimsy body, to be prevented from toying with its microscopic parts and holding them in front of the family's very eyes, before bringing it back to life so that it could continue on its way. The first one to get a handle on that device with the amplifier, the record and the needle that played the songs of Munir al-Mahdiyya and Zakariyya Ahmad; the first to introduce that machine to the town, which started to listen to it as it sat to alone on dresser tops. The first to create humans and animals out of materials that could easily repel jinns. He alone possessed that healing ability, that rejuvenating power over forces that no one could name or mention without fear. He wasn't a witch doctor, but something like a witch doctor. The important thing is that he ushered in a whole new era to the village. He was also the best looking of the young men: green eyes over the color of wheat were never before created with such beauty, and nobody else had such shiny shirts, which he had worn ever since learning the way to Haifa and showing up the other smugglers there with his street smarts and bravery. He was also the life of the party, with a voice that was powerful and emotive, like Zakariyya Ahmad's—the celebrity of the city, its greatest heartthrob, unrivaled lady-killer, the first in late-night soirees, the card player who never lost. He was also the drinker who never got drunk and the spendthrift who spent with abandon.

My father never knew days like those. For some reason, the higher his brother's star rose, the worse his own situation became. He nearly lost his scholarly edge. His cheerfulness lost its luster, and he got sick of those occasions when the elders challenged his intelligence. And, as if his family felt remorse because they had preferred him to his brother for so long, their concern for him lessened still more. He continued to come and go in the house at whatever hour he pleased without anyone's being concerned by his absence. Under the pretense that he had gained weight ever since going through puberty, they no longer hid sweets for him. He could sense all of this, and he wasn't pleased to have to fend for himself. The strange thing is that he didn't feel vindictive toward his brother. This comforted him—the consequences of a burdensome and gigantic superiority. He was truly glad and let himself fall behind in school, surrendering to long hours spent reading in bed. He was still a student, but his younger brother had money in his pocket and gave it to him freely so that he could live, spend money on his friends, buy books. His brother always gave without strings. He didn't carry a grudge from childhood, either.

Did my father feel freed from competition after his brother's death, or did he not have to wait that long? It's true that he was prudent and finished his baccalaureate after a month of solitary confinement, but he only did it so that he could stop there. He abandoned his studies and waited for his chance to teach primary school. He had his friends and his books, and he knew that, starting around then, nothing else of any great consequence would ever happen to him.

My uncle embarked on some massive undertakings with the fury of a storm: an extensive smuggling operation in and out of Haifa; running a movie theater; organizing concerts with the top singers of those days; opening a repair shop that specialized in pretty much everything; selling radios, sewing machines, and gramophones. He was always in Haifa or Beirut, returning with silk shirts, fine suits, and ties the likes of which none of the family had ever seen before. He was often accompanied by classy people who spent evenings at the bar and came home loaded. Lola, the infamous performer, liked to recount his exploits. That was more than the city could handle, more than the house could take, and, in particular, more than his father could handle. It became a real problem, especially after Lola, whose fame as a singer was matched only by her notoriety as a man-eater, got involved. His father was not accustomed to finding crowds outside his house. When he went inside, he was astounded to find this petite woman with lascivious eyes and full, painted mouth surrounded by men who lusted after her bare arms and exposed chest. What upset him even more, though, was the fact that his two daughters were delighted to be around a woman of such ill repute. He yelled at the girls to get out of there and then followed behind them. Maybe he expected his arrival alone to break up the gathering, so he waited for those present to scatter, but no such thing happened. Instead, he could hear high-pitched laughter, most likely from the sign of wonder, Lola. In the adjacent room, he heard his two banished girls crying. He shut the door, standing in half-darkness until his eyes adjusted, opened them, and then sat down even as his anxiety grew, certain of what had to be done. His anger was legendary, but anger is a voice and a glance, and in there he couldn't rely on his voice or his glance. He felt unable to get angry, like it was a waste of time to wait for the necessary anger as he sat alone there in the dark. Before encountering that woman, he had been afraid; at that moment he was even more afraid to walk out the door. He waited for a long time, until the blanket of stillness was lifted, before opening the door and breathing in the cool air, inhaling it deeply, as though he had just come to the surface from somewhere underground. No doubt the entire city spent that night and the following days gossiping about Lola and my uncle and the shame that had fallen upon my grandfather when he came home to find a mob congregating outside his door and gathering under his windows just to catch a glimpse of Lola. The sheikh and the effendi tiptoed around my grandfather's anger and took their sweet time in letting him articulate it, until the sheikh finally got him alone and told him how this whore was corrupting his house. The effendi goaded him until he finally mustered up the courage to walk in on Lola and his son—in one of his infamous tempers, cane in hand, brandishing it against everyone he saw. Lola burst out of the house screaming, her hair all a mess, with everyone chasing after her, singing bawdy songs as they pursued her through the alleyways and pressed their middle fingers against the nape of her neck—a kind of village custom practiced on newlyweds and musicians.

That was not the end. All the goings-on moved to a house on the outskirts of town, where the conversation returned once again to debauchery, magic, and drunkenness. One time after evening prayer, the sheikh mustered up his courage again and with his disciples in tow went to the bar and unleashed his cane upon the bottles of alcohol. He then proceeded immediately to the outlying house, but didn't find anyone there, so he doused the door with kerosene and set fire to the wood, leaving it to burn. It was promptly extinguished, but Lola never came back to Tyre. My uncle wasn't satisfied. The sheikh had many enemies in the city, and they welcomed my uncle as one of their own. It was their secret that the son of the sheikh's assistant was among their ranks. But it was other matters that really got to him—my uncle, that is: the near eradication of smuggling and the downfall of his business in a city that was too small to absorb such a hit. He carried on with his late-night debauchery until he could no longer afford to gamble. He went into debt and was forced to flee his debtors: moving from deception to lying, he even resorted to gambling with his partners' money and blackmailing his father and his sisters. This time the whole thing came to a head when his father booted him out of the house. So he left. His father waited patiently for some time before inviting him to come home again. The situation continued oscillating—between expulsion and return, return and expulsion—until he grew tired of it and felt the need to leave for good. So he left.

My father stayed out of what was happening to his brother as if he hadn't heard anything about his deteriorating state. He didn't talk to anyone about it except when absolutely necessary. When his father talked to him about it, he would listen without commenting, and when his father insisted on hearing his opinion, he replied, "Leave him be." He was lying in bed, as he spent most of his time at home, while his father stood over him and said that the situation was no longer tenable. He flipped his book over on its face and watched his father grow furious and menacing with his booming voice and his declarations. He always felt that the marble quality and eloquence of his father's voice sucked all meaning out of language. He stopped listening altogether until he sensed that his father had stopped talking. "Leave him be," he said, finding nothing better to say until he had the chance to think about it some more. It was not, of course, an occasion for revenge. His brother's deterioration would not make him a loser, but he didn't envy his brother as much as he envied him when he saw him like that, doing exactly what he wanted to do—building and destroying indifferently, sleeping with an older woman, her eyes greater than her stature, and half of her body exposed for everyone to see. This old sack of meat truly had become a jinn. He would certainly never catch up to his brother. Whatever he did, he wouldn't catch up. In his entire life, he would never accomplish as much as his brother was capable of in a single night. In the end, his brother eclipsed him without a chance of resurrection.

But did his brother really eclipse him, or did his truth simply shine through? Didn't his brother ever get tired of being compelled to outdo his own achievements every day, of being so clever, so spontaneous? Wasn't he being forced to struggle anew just to appear up to the challenge? Didn't his brother know that he was the one who didn't dare set foot in the bar? After all, he was the one who wasn't able to remain silent in front of the neighbor's wife, who, still in her bridal gown, as his two sisters watched, brazenly attacked him the night that had not been consummated yet. He couldn't raise his eyes to his father and leave the house that he had grown tired of and the city that he had grown sick of. All of that was too soon and too much for him, but it was within his brother's power on any given day. Then the neighbor's wife got bored with his brother and couldn't abide him for another day. She found him in the middle of the afternoon, heading for her room.

My father was rarely one to drink, but he went inside with Loverboy, who lived with his sister. The two didn't sit down until all the windows and doors had been closed. Loverboy served himself because it wasn't appropriate for him to offer alcohol to his sister. They both drank cheap wine because neither of them had the courage to drink arrack or real wine. They finished quickly, before anyone could walk in on them. They didn't drink too much, so they wouldn't appear drunk. Loverboy's sister wasn't concerned whether her brother behaved properly, but she used to interfere in his affairs without being asked. Without shame, she brought them food and more glasses, keeping them company in spite of her brother. She was young and beautiful and a widow only in name because the marriage hadn't lasted more than a week. The groom had been crushed beneath a giant boulder. She wasn't keen on going in bare-armed, walking up to the man with big eyes and telling him that the more he scowled, the more she could tell he needed a woman. She laughed hard, without worrying about what her brother might think, her brother who had always brought random women home with him and who she left alone with them in the only bedroom in the house. She used to tell him that her life was dry, and her eyes would turn pink, clearly revealing what she meant by that. Whenever my father knocked on her door while her brother was away, she welcomed him and invited him in with a strange insistence, fixed eyes, and an intoxicating voice—as if inviting him to enter her in the same way he had entered the house. But he pulled back, certain that he wasn't doing any of this as a courtesy to his friend, as he later told himself. She complained of a slight limp, which was barely noticeable, but he advised her to walk more slowly anyway. Loverboy's sister caught on and fought back a smile, as if warning him of something. He felt belittled by her insinuation. After that, he would allow his eyes to wander, to notice the limp, but only with difficulty and anxiety. This minor flaw started to make her look bad. She would never have noticed this limp if it hadn't been plain for all to see. And perhaps she wouldn't have received this kindness if he hadn't been underestimating her worth.

My father remembered his younger cousin's wife whom he had left with the family. She was an adolescent, beautiful and unlucky in marriage. She had approached him in the morning while he was still in bed and got in on the other side. He felt her tiny toes graze his. She waited for some small response from him, for him to jab his foot into her midsection, to reach his hand down and grab her foot. He didn't do either, and she left the very next day. When he grew tired of the memory and the regret and decided to propose to her, she didn't pay any attention to him; his chance had gone that morning. If his brother had been in his shoes, he would have done what was necessary; he wouldn't have feared the lame tip of a foot or kinship or anything like that; his brother definitely would have told his friend's sister and confronted his cousin's wife. But he himself didn't do anything. His clearest memories were precisely of those times when he didn't do anything. His brother wouldn't shy away from doing something even if it was going to destroy him. My father went on envying his brother for going out at night: gambling, drinking, and driving the most beautiful women in town to secluded locations or abandoned spots in the gardens. His brother increasingly profited off of him. My father didn't hold a grudge. He helped him with the money that began to make him crazy after he was formally appointed teacher and finally saved enough to send him to Dakar.

Did my uncle love Safia? She never talked to me about him. She just kept on saying how much I looked like him. I didn't know whether she was actually concerned about him or concerned about my father. I had always thought that I resembled my father, but as I got older, I discovered that my uncle was in my blood, that I had only resembled my father. From the moment I started down my uncle's path, I knew I would never stop.

After we came back from the cinema, we avoided touching one another. When my arm grazed hers in front of everyone, she didn't respond. She no longer wrapped her fingers around my hand or thrust her palm in my pocket or caressed my cheek with the back of her hand. Suddenly, all of those gestures vanished, and our entire relationship became discreet and evasive. We found being alone with each other unbearable and stopped meeting altogether, except when we were around her visitors, who weren't united by age or status: students, officers, and neophyte businessmen, party activists and students from classes that had just let out. More recently, the forty-something Naji, whom Hashim had invited, always seemed to be there. He was a journalist, and his presence made him a shining star in the village, which rarely hosted someone whose name was known beyond its own cafés. As usual, Hashim didn't consider what had been offered to him any more attractive than simply keeping his wife company. The fortyish bachelor didn't delay in seizing the opportunity. By our standards, he was a professional, and he didn't stop for very long to greet Hashim, instead hurriedly inviting Safia to spend the weekend with him in Beirut. The conversation could be seen and heard, but Safia wasn't surprised. She told him he was asking too much of her, but then recanted, asking him what he could offer her. No matter what he said, she always responded insouciantly, saying that it wouldn't be enough for her. When the game dragged on for too long, he stopped quoting figures and blurted out, "Don't be afraid, you won't come back disappointed." She understood what was going on before we did, threw a playful glance his way, and murmured through her teeth, "That's still not enough."

When I found her alone at home, I was sure that the possibility of reviving that moment at the cinema a week earlier had passed. Of course, I wasn't prepared: not then, not ever. I used to be able to put the moves on girls any way I liked, without improving my experience. We were satisfied with touching each other and were in that moment roused out of a desire by the fear that immediately came between us. I still haven't learned a damn thing.

She was still in the kitchen, and I didn't join her there. She left the kitchen, heading for her room, but I didn't follow her. She was in front of the mirror, quickly tying her hair back; I saw her hands coming together behind her neck, raising up her curls, and then returning to her face. She seemed to be doing that absent-mindedly, totally unmoved by my earlier advance. She certainly wasn't thinking about the moment we had come together or the week-old IOU I was looking to redeem just then with terrorlike trembling. Nothing about her had changed. I could tell that I was amusing to her, horny in some funny kind of way. I stumbled over myself, over my feelings. I couldn't even put on a halfway self-respecting face. As I stood in the living room, watching her raise her arms to her face, applying her makeup, I felt something like reprieve. From the room, she called, "Come over here. Don't just stand there." That was an order, so I obeyed. She was scrubbing her hair with a tissue that was collecting red powder. I had no doubt that the time was right, so I offered her a hundred hands. I didn't know where to put them. There was no place for them. They fell wherever they fell: blind, restive, rash. They fell in a funny way. I squeezed her close to me. I'm not sure how strongly I did that. I could tell by the look on her face that I did it harshly, but I didn't know what to do except go on squeezing. Caught between my hands that were clamped together like a vise grip, she was no longer able to move. I wanted her, all of her, up against me. Not just against me, but engraved in me. I wanted to be engraved in her, too. I pressed my lower half against her endlessly. I pressed her chest against me, and when I saw the wanton expression on her face, I squeezed her neck as hard as I desired. I felt her nose and her teeth collide with my face. It was my obligation, a costly part of the week-old claim, to kiss her, but I started losing the strength I had relied on, feeling that there was no reason to do so. Her open, parted mouth was in front of me, and I imprinted my mouth on hers. My mouth fastened itself to hers, my nose thrust in her face. I immediately pressed a different hardness against the hardness of her front. I was trying in vain to crush my body against hers. I pressed down on her mouth as though I were ridiculously welding our mouths together. Her lips parted, and I pushed through her teeth, through her saliva, and I felt something flow out of my mouth, drip down my chin. She sank her teeth into my tongue. The promised kiss dripped with saliva and intensity and pain. I loosened my grip, and she wrested herself from me, but didn't draw completely away. She stood calm, nonplussed, staring at me as she dripped with sweat and embarrassment.

My mother remained the foundation of the mourning for my uncle that went on in our home. When my father returned from Tyre, he seemed in good health to me, but my mother confided in us that he wasn't well. Everyone tiptoed around him to the point that at his school they gave him a special schedule; he would come and go with hardly any work. At home, he would eat a piece of bread with grilled ground meat and two potatoes twice a day at the same time: 12:30 and 8:30. He rarely spoke, and my mother reported to us whatever news she gathered inside that room the two of them shared at night. It was clear that he was overcoming something—a hiccup or a lump in his throat. He said it was nausea, something hovering over his heart and mind: visceral, painful feelings were at work deep inside him. He felt his stomach grinding, grinding all the time, and his heart beating, beating all the time, and his mind thinking, thinking all the time, and he couldn't handle any of it. My father used always to hear his body without being able to speak because the noise drowned out anything he said. He never said that he heard disturbances inside him that were unlike any other sound. He was stricken with fear every time his heart skipped a beat. He nearly choked whenever he felt his stomach pumping gas throughout his body, rising up to his shoulders. He never said that he could hear his own head while he was working or that what he actually heard was less like thoughts at all, but something more like the gears of a machine. Sometimes he heard his head inhale and exhale as though it were a lung. It wasn't a mental illness. The doctors believed the origin to be in his stomach. They gave him pills that he felt made his stomach work at a pace that the rest of his body simply couldn't keep up with.

My mother told us things my father said to her that we had never heard in our lives. She said he complained about our apathy and wished we would get interested in something. I found it hard to believe that my father became a different person when he was lying on his pillow. She wouldn't lie to us intentionally, but she was the kind of person who would believe anything he said. He couldn't understand how the truth might be otherwise. I don't know if she could tell the difference between things as they were and things as she wanted them to be. Maybe she just didn't imagine things could happen any other way. My mother didn't understand the connection between mourning and this unrealized desire to throw up, but she did understand that sadness had made my father ill and rendered him mute. She begged him to remain silent, to accept his thriving sadness; she also begged us not to speak, not to interrupt that sadness. Whenever someone tried to talk to him about his brother, she would advise that person to shut up because my father couldn't bear to talk or hear about him. Just like that, she could command total silence. We began to fear that if our tongues formed even a single word, it would wreck everything. In her permanent robe of mourning, my mother imposed a ban on us: against listening to the radio, pounding toys on the sidewalk, eating candy, celebrating holidays, wearing new clothes on holidays. She never went out, not for any reason. My father didn't have any relatives nearby, so this entire burden fell upon her, and she never hesitated once to take it on. The mourning had to be just so. Any mistake in the ceremony would have terrible consequences, and she made sure there were no screwups. She forgot about her own illness, that her heart was hanging by a thread; she never spoke of her own impending demise. Truth be told, her color had improved, and her face had filled out even if she continued to think, like the good wife that she was, that her husband's sadness was what really frightened her. To be a good wife or a good mother is to adhere to a set of rules: not to express any desire in her husband's presence, especially the desire to eat, drink, or go out. She dissimulated, pretending to eat with him so he wouldn't feel left out. Whenever he was around, it was tricky for her to go out; if he came home late, she had to wait patiently for him and not, under any circumstances, ask for anything for herself. She was prepared to live without sleep and without clothes if in the end she would still have her word and her reputation. She watched over everyone so they wouldn't leave her sight, but she lived in fear of finding that they had abandoned her. She wasn't comfortable around her husband's friends or her children; she didn't trust her neighbors and accused people continuously. As far as she was concerned, life was obligation, the mother's obligation and the wife's obligation, and there she was, carrying out the obligation of mourning.

After seeing my uncle off on a steamship, everyone had come back heavyhearted. His father didn't speak, and neither did my father. The two sisters talked until they got bored, like they did when their father ordered them not to mimic those bidding farewell by waving their handkerchiefs. Looking at their father's sullen face, the two sisters said that no one laughed in the house anymore. The younger one let out a giggle, but quickly clamped her teeth down on it as soon as her father glared at her. My father thought they were quite disagreeable, slow and pitiable in the absence of a brother who had seemed so elegant and unaffected on the steamship deck.

News of what was happening to my uncle continued to come in. He had become a tailor. Nobody knew that he had ever had any interest in tailoring. He took apart his suit, sewed it back together, and learned how to make suits. He spent two days at the tailor's and by the third day, noticing how the tailor made so many mistakes, set out on his own. He did very well for himself, and after a few short months he became tailor to the elite. When the French governor commissioned him to design a suit, he became the First Tailor of Dakar. As was his way, he went on to repair all sorts of things: watches, cars, radios, even irons. It's also said that he used to invent parts for watches and cars, that people started bringing him watches and cars that were in fine condition with the hope that he might give them back in even better shape. They grew accustomed to lateness and malfunctioning. He served all of Dakar, made a small fortune, and showered his financial bounty on the family. But his doting father didn't spend a cent of it until his younger daughter went insane, and he was forced to put her into an asylum. In fact, my aunt Ferial, whose name I only recently heard for the first time from my oldest aunt, didn't actually go insane. From a young age, she had been reckless, and at fifteen she ran off with a soldier. Fighting back his rage, my grandfather concluded that silence was preferable in such a situation. Despite his silence, two weeks later his friends noticed something different about him. One night a year later, that soldier showed up at his front door, and my grandfather, fighting back his rage a second time, followed him to find Ferial a prisoner of her own room one week after she had broken down. He carried her to the institution himself, but the arrangement didn't last, and she died right there on the spot. My aunt didn't say how, but she mentioned that my grandfather left it to his wife's family to transport Ferial to their cemetery. He forbid any memorial and never told the estranged brother, who had relied heavily upon her, what actually happened.

I didn't think of Safia very often until I learned that she went to Beirut with Naji. I couldn't blame her the more I thought about my uncle. I thought without really knowing what I was thinking about. It had to have been about nothing in particular, and I grew tired of thinking without knowing what I was thinking about. I hesitated to ask Safia after she had returned from her journey. I thought of Musa. Not only did Musa share my uncle's name, but he also looked a lot like him. My aunt had sent us pictures of my uncle's grave, and Musa was in almost every one of them: sitting on top of the grave itself, his large body at the headstone, the Qur'an open between his legs as he gazed off toward the horizon. There was no overstatement in these pictures—just Musa looking out toward the horizon from atop the burial site as if gazing from the balcony of his house. My aunt said that Musa was my uncle's friend, but there was something about what she said that made no sense to me. Something she never spoke of had interrupted that friendship. I had never seen a picture of my uncle, though I later found an old one after my father died. His ban on pictures of my uncle was finally lifted when it was no longer possible for him to ban anything. My father's accidental death seemed like punishment for the mourning that had dragged on for a long time, like a door eternally open to death. I had never seen a picture of my uncle, and all old photos look alike to the extent that those in them no longer resemble themselves. In this sense, it seemed to me that the only picture of him left was that one of Musa on top of the grave, reading. In one picture, Musa is standing up, regarding the grave without sadness. His pointy chin, wide eyes, and thick lower lip are visible. But his confusion is also visible, his arms dangling at his sides. And the strangest thing of all is that subtle difference between his hands. I imagined them to be of two different sizes and then noticed that one of them was missing something. Upon closer inspection, I could make out that it was a stump of two or three fingers or perhaps even nothing more than the butt of his palm.

In another picture, Musa appears to have completely forgotten his left hand while his right cradles a book. In some surreal way, the left palm seems to be covered with a solid, glossy material that I assumed was a leather glove he used to wear in order to hide some grotesque deformity in his fingers.

I asked my aunt about Musa. She couldn't tell me anything about him with any certainty. She told me that he was the nephew of an early immigrant to Abidjan. He had moved when he was still a child and grew up there; or maybe he had actually been born in Dakar. She said he got married and had nothing but daughters, a lot of them—five or six or seven, she couldn't recall anymore. But as time went by, his life and his wife turned into one big argument. "He's always been hard," my aunt said. "He's been corrupted by his grandfather Sheikh al-Deeb's family, all of whom have this strange disposition, prone to spending long hours without seeing anyone." She knew that Musa had been around here for months, perhaps since his family—his daughters and his sons-in-law—had ganged up on him and kicked him out of his own house. Or perhaps since they had presented him with a bizarre proposition: leave his work and his family and go to Lebanon to live in a room under the stairs, insane or halfway there.

He prayed and recited *du'a* and went fishing with dynamite. A strange hobby for someone from a family with no fishermen in it, yet somehow they managed to pass that hobby down from father to each and every son. They used to say that he wasn't right in the head and that he simply needed to be left alone. The weird thing was that not even my aunt ever tried to find him. I'd bump into him on the street or in the marketplace. He didn't have the same face I knew from the pictures of him. It now seemed to belong to somebody else. It was the same length, but the appearance had changed somehow. Not only his age, but every idiosyncratic expression was trapped behind that taut flesh. He still had an exaggerated ordinariness that made him both familiar and forgettable at the same time, as if his face could have belonged to anyone, as if he had been manufactured in a prison, I thought, seeing him—to my astonishment—coming toward me from the market stall. He reached out his hand, which I noticed was not covered by a glove; the ancient, dry skin itself was like a weapon. I also noticed scarred pockmarks on his face. He began to apologize, though for what I wasn't quite sure, perhaps for being curt and for learning of my father's death so long after the fact. I also felt as if I had to apologize for matters no less ambiguous. He called me "the son of the beloved." I didn't understand what he meant by that exactly. Full stops followed his bewildering expressions. He went on rambling, repeating over and over that I was "the son of the beloved" until he got teary-eyed over something I couldn't understand. He looked like a quivering armadillo, and on his ordinary face I glimpsed a strange look of pity. "May God give you strength," he mumbled and then released my hand. When he turned around, I noticed two brawny forearms bulging out of his short sleeves.

"Come on over here," he said, spinning around and continuing to walk. As my estrangement from Safia dragged on, I thought more about his visit, but I couldn't find the strength to pursue him. Like curiosity masquerading as desire, something had transformed my uncle's absence into loss. Was that "thing" desire for Safia? I could never admit it to myself. The second time I saw Musa, I immediately headed toward him even as he remained as silent as a corpse. And when his hand, with which he forgetfully continued to shake mine, started getting warm from what I was doing to it, I saw the bewilderment return to his face after a quick flicker of consciousness lit up in his eyes, but was then extinguished. I said good-bye to him, but as soon as I moved a few steps away, I sensed him turn, as if to flee, and I was surprised to hear a strange voice in the middle of the market say, "Come on over here."

Once the incident had passed, my father began to talk about my uncle as though he had forgotten him. Those memories structuring the anxiety of being forgotten turned into a kind of forgetfulness in the end. An obituary made all of that into a legacy that was impossible to calculate and led to the squandering of most of that legacy in an attempt to protect it. My father remembered only the headlines: his father's skills, his esteem for him. I don't know if he ever knew whether his brother became bored with the heresy of watches and suits. His brother definitely had broader horizons before him. He thought about building a factory and had actually found a partner to do so with him, but he soon fell under the siren song of diamonds.

At first, he had been told that the enterprise would require more than just a straw hat and a few cents for African representation. He actually did buy a hat and spent more than a few francs because the French who supported the Africans were wealthy. In the end, they granted him broad tracts of land, and when he went to check them out, he discovered that they were actually a village, a village replete with fields and rolling hills and houses and a river, and that it was up to him to get things started. The village head welcomed him in his hut, addressing him in a language he didn't understand. He realized afterwards that the head-man had comprehended what was said and that he both understood and was able to speak French better than my uncle, who still wasn't proficient. He wasn't the first person to be received by the village head. Many had come before him, and he appraised their gifts before granting them by his authority a piece of land on the riverbanks in the jungle. My uncle was given a piece of land whose earth was unsuccessfully excavated, so one night after his black workers had skipped out on him, he simply left it the way it was. That was enough of a bad omen, but my uncle never gave it a second thought. He had turned twenty-six a few days earlier, and nothing could faze him. He tried cobbling together enough black workers to dig on the riverbanks, but he came up short, and he was forced to return to the village sheikh with even more gifts to secure the necessary number of men. He understood that he had to offer gifts to the village god directly or else elicit his wrath, thereby scaring off the workers. This cost my uncle a great deal and prevented him from owning anything more than his hat. But he quickly found new partners who had faith in him at a time when no one trusted anyone. They funded him. He needed to fence off his plot, but that was pointless because borders didn't truly become real there until the spirits had blessed them. He had to return yet again to the village sheikh, who had just finished celebrating with his family by slaughtering four calves on all four sides of the village, before the witch doctor could begin his special rites, leaving a share for the god of lightning, another for the god of wind, and a third for the god of rain. Afterwards, the spirits danced underneath masks and delimited the sacred boundaries; the witch doctor inscribed the totemic symbol of the village in blood on my uncle's forehead and cajoled him into dancing with the people of the village after removing his shirt and hat, which the witch doctor proceeded to hide among the crowd.

The boundaries were drawn, but the matter didn't end there: his white neighbors didn't respect each other's borders, especially those that had been drawn along the riverbanks, and many of the blacks didn't believed in a village god who was flexible on matters of theft. He had to leave a share for the thieves and for their god who recognized no boundaries. If he took too long, the supplies would be stolen, at which point he would have to return to the same formula—from village sheikh to witch doctor, as well as to the thieves' sheikh and their god.

He would have gone broke again had they not brought him the first diamond. He didn't expect it to happen so quickly. He was on the verge of giving up when he realized, beyond a shadow of a doubt, that he wouldn't be able to control anything there, even though his workers—who he feared might steal his supplies and even the shirt off his back—brought him that diamond, placed it in his hands.

It dawned on me that Safia was the reason I was constantly thinking about my uncle these days. My thinking about him was like a search for her. I wasn't surprised to find her in our house. My absence was particularly effective when I was able not to think about it. I had summoned her in some way. She said, "I was starting to get bored; I've been here for two hours already." Something about her hair, her robe, made her seem younger. She followed me into the bedroom. I could feel her behind me. That's when she put her hands on my shoulders.

"Run your fingers through my hair. Not like that. Slowly. Spread your fingers apart and pull slowly. Don't press down too hard on my scalp. Stroke it gently. Don't just repeat the same motions over and over. Don't repeat them like a machine either. Don't drift away from me now" (at this point, I was thinking about letting my hands wander). "The kissing lesson will be even harder; don't push it now." I was always losing control. My body was always getting ahead of me. I had to restrain it, to change myself into a clock, to set my body to the second, even though there somehow always seemed to be a one-second delay that ruined everything. An invisible pressure. But the movement itself might become aggression with the slightest change. Torturous rhythms. Maybe I simply have to kill my own movement, to do absolutely nothing with this body that is always getting ahead of me. She really was patient with me. And when things were finally going well, she rewarded me with a soft embrace. She got undressed. I had to adjust my body to her rhythms. It was not like learning to walk. My body was idiotic and annoying. There I was with these two legs, and I couldn't even get one of them into the right position, not even for a moment. Maybe it would have been easier if I had only one leg. "Get your chest off of me. Your hand's on my breast. Grab it all, but don't squash it. Now grab the other one." She suddenly pulled her head back and moved away from me. She tossed me up and sent me flying. I rose above her like a volleyball player hovering above the net as she raised herself to me at precisely the right moment. I rocked back and forth as she inclined her body toward me. I was up in the air, and it actually felt as if a cool breeze were wafting over me. Something enjoyable, enjoyably pleasurable, gave me stamina this time. Then an unexpected blow brought me down, and I could no longer tell if I was up in the heavens or down on earth.

I thought of my uncle. He certainly wouldn't have needed lessons like this. Still, I walked away from the experience resembling him even more. When Safia got out of bed and walked naked over to the mirror, I was impressed by her tight buttocks. In their applelike shape, there was a wholeness that gave the rift running between them an incredible appeal. I saw a trace of me on her shoulder. I was amazed that I had been able to do that without her noticing. I assumed that I had come. I was fully conscious throughout, leaving my body only for a moment, so how had I not noticed my own ejaculation? The whole time I had been thinking not about her or about myself, but about my uncle. I had grown very close to him there, without ever knowing his face. I could detect him all around me. His evocative desire was both the anthem of my own desire and the anthem of my body. I needed him in order to deserve having that woman. After making love, I was actually able to feel my body, as though it were a precious vessel I had to respond to. I pictured him penetrating her so that I could imagine myself doing the same. I imagined him on top of her, and I got hard just thinking about it. His lust was my invisible strength, the shadowy power that inspired me. Did she think about him while she was making a man out of me? Did she think about his hand on her body, about his penetrating her? Did she think of him while I was thinking of him? It occurred to me that it had become fair game for me to ask her about him and that she, like me, could sense his presence in the room with us.

I pulled my body back, threw my head down on the bed, and collapsed against the solidity and coolness of the wood. I felt as if I were pulling myself upwards, to a greater height. After making love, I was free in this body that was almost ready to come back recharged. Without thinking, I asked her if she had loved my uncle. "I liked him," she said, as if banishing any conversation about love. I pulled the clip out of her hair, but she didn't turn toward me, hurrying instead to put my clothes back on: "They'll be here any minute." I buttoned my shirt and went to wait for her in the living room. She soon joined me, but sat down far away. When she felt me looking at her, her expression changed, as if she was offended by what lingered on my face from the union that had connected us just a moment before. Suddenly, without wasting any time, she said, "Your eyes are playing tricks on you." She got up and disappeared into the kitchen. I didn't hear a sound out of her and waited longer than I thought was possible. Then it occurred to me to go to the door that she was slowly moving behind and strained my ear toward her, before ducking in and shutting it behind me.

I don't know why my uncle had left nothing but silent people in his wake. When I met with Musa that same day as he was emerging from his lair, he insisted that we go back to his room. We descended the four stairs, and I immediately found myself in front of a low door. When Musa turned the light on, I saw nothing but uneven concrete bareness on the ground, walls splotched with coarse, greenish cement. It was almost as if everything there were a single color—the bed folded up in the corner, the gas stove that he eagerly tried to light as soon as we arrived, the wooden futon covered with a tattered mattress—a color lagging behind all others. Light didn't eradicate the sense that the essence of the things there lived in darkness and private isolation. The faint scent of putrescence added to that essence. Still, the place wasn't filthy. Just the opposite—there was something about it that was like the hygiene of a prison. Musa kept on trying to light the stove and then placed a rusting zinc kettle on it. He went back to lamenting the loss of his father, and I felt as though, in this way, he was avoiding talking about my uncle. I asked him, "And my uncle?" He wasn't ready, wavering for a moment before finding a response, "Your uncle, God bless him." I asked him how he had died; he said he didn't know. At the time, Musa had been in the country, and, when I saw him in the photo, I figured it was all in his head the whole time. When I asked him if he ever met my uncle's fiancée, Safia, he told me that he hadn't even known he was engaged. He answered definitively. And when I voiced my amazement that he didn't know his friend was engaged, he replied, "We were just relatives." "But weren't you friends?" Without hesitation, he answered, "No, we were just relatives." I asked him what my uncle had looked like, and he answered, "Some say he was handsome." "But you don't think so?" "It doesn't matter," he said. I asked him how they met; he said he couldn't remember. I asked him what he used to do in Dakar, and he replied, "We used to do everything."

When I told my aunt what Musa had said, she didn't comment. I asked her, "How could he have been his friend without knowing anything about him?" She said, "And what gave you the impression that they were friends?" I said, "The pictures, he was in all of those pictures you sent of my uncle's grave." She said, "But I didn't send any pictures of your uncle's grave." I asked her, "Haven't you prayed at his grave?" "That was his custom," she replied. "When he got upset, he prayed over every grave." I pulled myself together and asked her about Safia. She stared back with eyes aflame and said, "Your uncle never talked to anyone. That whore clung to him. She left her fiancée and clung to him. Her father was his partner and didn't want any problems with him. She forced herself on him. . . . " She reached the peak of her frightening anger and thrust her eyes and nose in my face, shouting, "Let me tell you! That whore ain't gonna rest. She wants to drag you down with her. She ain't gonna rest."

His partner. What a partner. Ali Sharaf was no ordinary rich person. People speak of markets named after him in Dakar, of property he owns all over the world. He could have been a leader of the community in Dakar if he had wanted to or became a member of Parliament if he had answered the call of the political bosses who wanted him on their electoral lists during each and every election cycle. But he wasn't interested. He was no hedonist either. He left his second wife to go live in a palace in Casablanca with her two daughters and two children from his previous marriage. He let them live however they wished, but they chose to hole themselves up in their palace, rarely stepping outside, sending drivers and servants to take care of everything. That isolation made their home a suspicious place even before the murdered servant was found. The police had evidence that the killer was one of the house drivers, and even though the crime was barely more than an accident, it had dramatic repercussions. The family couldn't bear to stay, so they left Morocco. This time, Ali Sharaf sent them to France. He didn't object when Safia told him she wasn't going along.

Ali Sharaf was not a model of wealth. His house was big, but he never cleaned it. He left that to the servants, who dragged their feet, but without his ever really noticing. His infrequent visitors were often surprised by the disorderliness of the house, finding cigarette ash and even burning embers on the rugs and the couches. Nevertheless, he walked around barefoot sometimes or with no shirt on, perhaps having a spot of fun with them by swatting at flies or playing with his toes. For the most part, he left them alone and disappeared somewhere in the house. The strange thing was that money seemed to flood in without his doing much of anything. The times when his agents or his partners tried stealing from him didn't last. He threw them out without confrontation and without their even knowing how he found out they were up to no good. An aimless wanderer, a stammerer, half-stoned, he didn't keep account books, but had everything carefully filed away in his head. The others usually got bored of his rambling, of his being lured away by something else, and had a hard time focusing his attention on a single topic. He was distracted easily; his incomplete, dismantled sentences collapsed, and he left midway through conversations, a blank expression on his face, rushing off to anywhere else.

Ali Sharaf was a creature of the night. He wouldn't get out of bed before sundown and stayed up all night making model buildings and ships, waiting for inspiration to come to him. The old hunter couldn't read very well, but spent his nights hard at work, poring over those two yellowing volumes of magic. He tried to make a magic carpet and an invisibility cap so he could cross the ocean to find the elixir of eternal life, to discover the land of eternal youth. In the basement of his house, there were piles of feathers and potions with acrid odors, alembics and lots of lead and bones, triangles, circles, ropes and threads, carpets, broad umbrellas, gears and knobs and powder, nails and cymbals. He prepared all of it in consultation with his two books. Still, he wasn't successful because there were some necessary ingredients that simply couldn't be found, either on earth or in the heavens above. He abandoned alchemy but didn't give up on magic. He went to the jungle to learn from the witch doctors, where he acquired the ability to converse directly with spirits and to manipulate mysterious powers, even without a magic carpet.

My uncle met him during ritual celebrations in the jungle but didn't speak to him, thinking of him more as one of the witch doctors. When the celebration was over, my uncle took the feather and the bones from him and drove his car to the city, or, rather, he invited himself to Ali Sharaf's house, which stood on a giant, shrouded hill, bedecked with arches and long verandas and expansive chambers filled with large furniture. My uncle weaved through those salons alone after his host disappeared. He wandered for an hour, amazed, passing from room to room as if he were spinning in the vortex of a single room that he couldn't find his way out of. A room in a room, a Bedouin tent in a Bedouin tent. It was like a trap. After a while, my uncle felt that this emptiness couldn't be real and that what sounded like moaning couldn't possibly have been. It occurred to him that the palace was breathing, murmuring like a living organism. He was horrified by the thought that he was trapped inside some terrible beast. He didn't see anyone, as if he had been left alone on purpose. He continued putting one foot in front of the other until he approached what appeared to be the central room. He heard a commotion coming from the corner and found himself in a spacious kitchen filled with a slew of servants who were either uninterested in his question about where his host was or didn't hear the question in the first place. They offered him fruit and a stiff drink. His fear receded, and he headed back the way he had come in. He was still searching for the door when he noticed two narrow, shining eyes observing him through a door that led to one of the bedrooms. It was Safia.

The young lady told him he was as far away from the exit as he could possibly be. In front of him, there was an entrance to the garden. She took him by the hand to give him a tour, showing him the interior of the palace, which to his astonishment he noticed was actually a chain of houses. He could see gorgeous rooftops, balconies, and cozy little huts. It was a hodgepodge of architectural styles and multiple tastes. In addition to that ominous-looking palace, he identified various Arabic, African, and Moorish influences, several schools of design, and more than one world, all under the same roof. Most doors led places he could never dream of! A deception: trap doors that led nowhere! My uncle was getting tired, but the young lady who had sneaked into his thoughts told him not to be afraid, that it wasn't a magic palace, just very old. Rulers, tribal leaders, thieves, and foreigners had lived in it before. She thought they all were mad. She suggested they take a rest together on the balcony overlooking one of the palace's gardens. He had no idea where the servant who offered him coffee had come from, but the young lady who had been dispatched to sit him down somewhere was obviously used to seeing the African sunset from there. She said she didn't know where to find her father. The only person who might know was a servant whom all the other servants were afraid of; they said he was a witch doctor. She couldn't find that servant right then anyway.

She didn't talk very much. Speaking didn't seem to be her preferred medium of expression. She said much more with her eyes; from her eyes alone her stubbornness, her independence, and her fear could be discerned. She went on in her weepy voice, speaking in a passive and absent form—a language without a subject. My uncle was not one of those who could handle searching too much beyond words, but the twang in her voice soothed him. Not just her accent, but also the weakness of her expressions, which seemed to him like a physical handicap, eliciting his tenderness and support, making him feel as if he were drowning her with his incessant talking, overpowering her. His way of speaking didn't soothe her. His flood of words startled her, like a sudden heavy downpour. She was unable to protect herself from him. He was a man of the world, someone sent to keep her company, and she was compelled to accept his outstretched arm. In actuality, when she demurely told him that she had been in the same place for two months without leaving, he proposed that she leave with him. She didn't say no.

The two of them went on talking while the sunset proceeded as if the earth were liberating itself from a fever with one powerful breath. The trees were released, and the air itself appeared to be listening for some imperceptible language, roaming like a live breath, while the ghostly jungle rose toward the giant moon, which showed itself briefly like a tattoo on the skin of the sky. Was that *the* African sunset? Suddenly, they spotted Ali Sharaf staring down at them from the corner of the balcony, looking without seeing them, and then disappearing in the blink of an eye.

She said she hadn't left there since her mother, Sara, had departed for Paris, but she crossed the threshold with my uncle by her side and went with him to houses, dance halls, and pubs. Wherever they went, there were fun crowds, drinking, and dancing. The whole city was in the palm of his hand, as though he were the maestro of late-night parties organized by him and his sons. He offered her his wing, and she accepted to be underneath it. It was enough for her simply to find a chair beside him while he talked, joked, and sang songs. She wasn't interested in participating. She wasn't Lebanese, Moroccan, Senegalese, or French; she didn't have a mother tongue or a street language. She was fluent in Arabic, French, Spanish, and more than one African dialect, but she couldn't tell a joke in any of them. She was a foreigner in every language everywhere she went. She hated speaking so much. She felt that the more she spoke, the more she was translating from one language to another in her head. She told my uncle all of this, but he didn't seem to understand, to find anything particularly wrong with it. He seemed to make her giddy for him. She was around many people, but she was only truly with him. Only to him could she speak without being self-conscious, without being concerned whether he understood everything she said. Perhaps she noticed that when he didn't understand, he didn't enjoy cracking his head open to understand. It didn't bother her.

I didn't sense Safia's anger, but I was angry with myself anyway. She was sitting with her guests, dressed in a low-necked white dress, and her lustrous hair was up. To her right was that activist who hadn't been over to her house for a long time. He went right back to cracking jokes, showing off his arrogance more than his wit. I came in without saying hello and made straight for an unoccupied chair, but she got up and kissed me. She left where she had been sitting and came to sit next to me. She held my hand and flirtingly read its lines, all but saying that it was the hand of an asshole who, after having conquered her, would simply abandon her. "Where were you two days ago? You thought you could just run away like that? You shithead. You don't even deserve me." She spoke in a raised voice, and those seated all around her laughed heartily. I laughed, too, and she could tell that in my inebriated state I would be capable of making fun of the activist, who didn't manage to stop me; he probably felt his wit wouldn't be able to protect him after all, and after asking permission, he left. She told me in something between a whisper and a shout, loud enough for those both near and far to hear, "We had to keep you in the dark. We'd lost you. You grew up in such a hurry, young man. We just couldn't include you anymore." Her eyes, her chest, her lips, everything about her washed over me; her joke was part of this outpouring. I wasn't supposed to interrupt that, not even with a single word. It was supposed to be enough for me just to accept, to accept the joy of this expression to my flesh. I couldn't hear very well anyway. I felt the words—whether whispered or laughed—like little indentations pressed in the shape of her lips.

I heard Hashim talking to me; he had sidled up to me without my even noticing. I suspected that he got close to all of Safia's boyfriends, turning her and himself on in the process. He had tried to arrive at lunch before me. I backed off at his enthusiasm, and he finished eating before me and went to take a nap. As I was putting the last of the plates away in her kitchen cabinets, Safia put it aside and took off one rubber glove, leaving her other hand near the surface of the water. She placed her hand on my chest, sliding across its hair, down to my stomach. I pulled her toward me and embraced her. She grabbed me with her still-gloved hand, but when she noticed that I was hard, she pushed me away and went back to caressing my chest hair. A moment later she went back to arranging her cabinets. I was standing in a corner of the living room when she fell against the door, took off her apron, and let down her hair. Some time passed before she looked at me. Something in her long, narrow eyes snapped, something deep, and I could sense that it was generations older than me. It was also dull, albuminous, subdued. I looked at her whitish face, the unblemished cream-colored skin, so close yet so far, seeming to be perpetually behind a diaphanous veil, suspended in its own moonless night—that arresting cream color flecked with the purest olive. For the first time, I noticed crows' feet tugging at the corners of her eyes, wrinkles at the base of her cheek, between her eyes. I found them all incredibly sexy. They reminded me of her body's curves, which I saw when we were in bed together, the curves I had considered signs of maturity and wholeness that required generations to develop. All of a sudden something occurred to me. The color of her face was exactly the same color as semen: bronze, creamy, egg white. I thought of how it also had the same aroma—dough and eggs. How the smell of semen is the smell of fertility flowing down from days gone by.

I thought of my uncle. I thought that Safia's face and perhaps mine as well were the color of albuminous fertility. I had inherited that semenous color from him. I was lying on my side with Safia in a house that I had rented from a student who was also a relative of mine. A room with a bed, a floor mat, and a gas stove. She had thrown off her coat, disrobed, and jumped on top of me. On top of her and inside her, I felt once again as if I had a recently liberated body, an unexpected gift beyond all imagination. Or a gift from generations, both living and dead. And why not a gift from my uncle too? This awesome woman carried me toward him, as if giving birth to me or to him during every moment of intercourse. I looked at her while I was on top of her. She had this face, broken with desire, that effused from some other time or maybe from some other man. I stroked her wet pubic hair. I felt her face was my own. I inhaled my nectar, my elixir. Here, my blood and his mingled in such a way that it was no longer foreign to me, with every thrust she pounded me, bringing me deeper inside her. Channels of blood and seminal passageways returned me to him and to my father. I suddenly asked her if he was smart. There was no need to mention his name. "You're smarter than he was," she replied. I asked her if he was handsome. "You look like him," she said. She backed away a little, rested on her elbow, and asked me, "Why do you ask about him so much?" "What's weird about me asking about my uncle? He was my dad's brother." "You don't look like him," she said. "You don't look like him," she repeated. *I don't look like him?* This didn't strike me as strange. I already knew that somehow. I placed her palm on my cheek and slowly rubbed it against me. Then, as if making sure of something, she said, "You're a nice person."

Nice indeed. Wasn't my uncle nice? Didn't he bring her home before midnight and say good night to her at the door? They would have been waiting for him at the party, especially those blondes who always seemed to show up whenever something was going on between him and some other girl. She was one of those girls, and as far as that group was concerned, she was still Ali Sharaf's prisoner. She was there for something like a trial period. How it pleased her when he leaned over her wearing a fine cologne and lightly grazed her cheek before she headed off to her room. From the time that she was eight years old, she had begun to notice boorish, well-connected men slipping into her mother's quarters. When that big-lipped servant was killed, she understood that the insane driver had lost his mind for some reason unrelated to her mother. That same driver had squeezed Safia's breasts repeatedly with his thick hands before she had even developed breasts. She used to love how my uncle said good-bye to her, but the thought of him returning to the party, to the blondes, started to bother her. She began using every excuse in the book to make him stay, but he rarely did. She still didn't understand how her father managed to appear whenever she came home accompanied by my uncle, only to disappear a moment later. She would lie awake listening to my uncle and wouldn't fall asleep until he stopped moving. She didn't find him there in the morning because he used to get up very early, no matter where he fell asleep. She waited two or three days until she heard from him. She just waited; she never grew tired of waiting. Waiting starts out terribly, but then turns into a kind of sick hope. She always feared that he might never come back. While she waited, she would forget how he hardly ever read books and never understood what she said or sometimes didn't even hear her. He was a mediator between her jokes and her conversation with the party girls, sitting perfectly still, as if he was with her for no other reason than to save his energy and his conversation for some other occasion.

His presence began to hurt her. She had never experienced this kind of pain, nor had she ever been interested in making anyone or anything stay with her. She didn't know what real pain was. When she learned that she was going with her mother to Casablanca, far away from Dakar, she searched her feelings but found none and went to sleep. She slept for two nights straight, and when she woke up, she was edgy, impatient, and went right back to sleep. She was like that for a month or more and couldn't stop until she had recovered from this condition. In her sleep, she used to confront everything that was troubling her. When that lush of a driver plopped his giant hands down on her chest, she couldn't hear a sound. He kept sliding his hands all over her petite body until she heard snoring coming out of her open mouth. She didn't know when this sleeping condition started. Maybe after she saw her father dragging her limp and dumbfounded mother by the hair, pick up the doorstop—a large stone slab—and hold it up in his hands. On that day, she saw her mother's eyes widen to the point of becoming pure white. She was blind, facing down that stone he was about to slam down on her. Then she screamed, screamed loud, and passed out. Her father's hands went limp, while Safia—fast asleep—saw a giant bird lift up the stone. Then she saw her mother on a table, a doll made out of twenty-four separate pieces. At first, she counted twenty-four, but then found only twenty-three. She recounted them, finding twenty-three, but couldn't figure out what had happened to the missing piece. Then she felt certain she would find it in her father's storehouse. But she was also afraid that she wouldn't find it. Then she counted twenty-five pieces, saying that she must have taken something very precious from her father's dresser.

Safia was afraid that sleep would overtake her on this occasion as well. How could she protest if she was asleep? That night, although she was afraid my uncle might still be out with the blondes, she shook off the grogginess that had started to caress her eyelids and waited, half-asleep. When he came home, she checked him for foreign odors and nearly fell asleep in his arms, but she was able to fight it off without falling over. When she finally gave in to the possibility of sleeping, she was unable to do so. She stayed awake, wide-awake, until sleep finally took her. Awake—the life she was living had been completely transformed into pain. She could feel her body's circulation. Her entire body was manufacturing this pain. The weight on her chest, her constricted throat made it so that she could breath only with great effort. She was terrified of herself for half an hour. Where did all of this come from? She thought it was something that only death would bring to an end. In fact, she fell silent waiting for death, waiting for anything. But she woke up repeatedly, about once a minute, and each time she inspected her chest before going back to sleep. It was hard for her to see herself clearly: half-strangled, microscopic workers were trying to unclog her plumbing, working in her head and her arteries with jackhammers that nobody else could hear. And so, during that African winter, at eighteen years of age, Safia discovered the honor of pain.

She chose pain over sleep. Of course, she had every right to choose. She kept herself awake in pain to prevent losing him, to prevent losing herself in sleep. She spent white nights wide-awake until she started craving sleep. Sleep wouldn't do her any good, though, if it simply converted her pain into a nightmare. She would never get accustomed to that, no matter how long it lasted. During his rare appearances, Ali Sharaf didn't say a word to her, but she knew that he knew. Nothing got past him, she knew, despite his idiosyncrasies. Would he have sent her mother to Casablanca if he hadn't known? Didn't he know everything about her mother once she was in France? Doubts came over Safia that he might have arranged everything from there, but he was the one sending her mother those boorish men in the form of servants and drivers. He wasn't far removed from what had gone down in Casablanca under her mother's protection. In all like-lihood, that was a warning her mother had understood, and so her daughters moved away from her, terrified of what might happen.

Musa was at the door on that *khamasin*-filled morning that kept my mother and me corralled in our rooms. I hadn't seen that straw hat he was wearing since I was a child. In my memory, I always associated him with shorts or golf pants. Musa was standing right in front of me, wearing a ratty shirt that didn't hide the smooth, solid strength in his broad shoulders and arms. There was a faint scar on his cheek; I couldn't remember if I had ever noticed it before. It added a kind of seediness to his expressionless face that was made worse by the coarse hair on his unshaven chin, the obligatory component of a religious education. But what really grabbed my attention were his eyes, which had widened beneath the taut skin of his face. They sparkled and danced as though they didn't belong to him, as if they were his prisoners. In my own head, I distinctly heard one of those comments that occasionally cause me to think: "He's a dead man." I was a little bit unnerved, as I always am whenever I hear voices in my head. I didn't remember hearing Musa's voice. Maybe he had broken a few letters in his mouth or strung several words together.

When he came in, I welcomed him into the salon, which at that moment was a bit like a waiting room. Musa threw himself on the nearest couch like a weary traveler. He said he had been in the neighborhood and wanted to see me. Why did he bother coming at all if he was forced to lie like this? My mother offered him an over-the-top welcome, as was her custom, with one of her husband's colognes. She sat down melodramatically, and I felt her presence weighing on the meeting, but I succeeded, with some difficulty, in getting her to leave. Once she left, he loosened up a little, but still wasn't quick to speak. A moment later he blurted out, "Why are you asking about your uncle? The man passed away a long time ago. Leave him alone. Leave things between him and his God." I didn't have an answer since I myself didn't even know why I asked about him. I didn't know if I was searching for him, for Safia, or for my father. I ended up saying that he was my uncle, my father's brother, and that I deserved to know as much as I could about him. He said to leave the dead to their God. No one but God knows the nature of Man. I thought about the profane language encapsulated in that single phrase, how it commanded silence, how it insisted on no response. Without budging, he cantankerously asked, "What's the point . . . what?! They're gone, with all their good and all their ill. Why must we disturb the dead in their graves? We have no right digging up secrets in this way. Its shameful and inappropriate for a nice boy like you. Show your uncle some respect and leave him alone." I sensed that he was very angry. This amazed me. Without saying much of anything, he had said more than was necessary, but he didn't have the strength to finish. I tried asking him what he had meant by "secrets" and "digging," but he didn't reply—as if his speech had been exhausted and there wasn't another single word left in his throat.

He fell back into his reverie and left me confused, sitting in the chair, unsure of what to do with myself. My mother came back in and found us like this, so she started up once again with the perfunctory pleasantries. He remained distant until he raised his glazed eyes to hers, and she left us again for her kitchen. A very long moment passed as my patience for this whole scene ran out. He got up and headed toward the door. I let him go, but when he reached it, he cast me an arrogant look up and down and, taking a step away, said, "Stay away from Safia."

So he knew Safia after all. Why had he denied it before? Safia had said that he was nobody special to her. My uncle had brought him in and made him a partner. He was loyal and trustworthy, and when that tree fell on him, they thought he might not pull through. He lived, but at the expense of losing his mind. He became hostile and confrontational, and in the end neither his wife nor his daughters could put up with him anymore. After my uncle's death, Safia stopped receiving word from Musa. To this day, she still doesn't know who got him to Lebanon. Everyone who told me about Musa said that he had come in a state of manic excitement. They would always see him on the coast, night and day, in the cold and wind, without daring to go up to him. Those young men who tried it encountered a great deal of violence and arm strength. He spent a whole year like that. Neither the cold nor the madness destroyed him. Then an extraordinary feeling of peace descended upon him. He no longer had a sense of touch or the power of speech or any other expression; it was as if he were dead. He didn't exhibit any signs of madness in the pictures I had seen of him at the grave. I repeatedly asked my aunt about them, but she stood by her story: What pictures? I rifled through the boxes in which my dad had kept his papers but didn't find any pictures. I realized that they must have been hidden. I asked my mother about it, but she didn't respond. Then I found a letter among my dad's papers that brought everything together. A bizarre letter expressing a great nervousness: "Forgive me, Master, my thoughtlessness and my ignorance. I am my own worst enemy . . . I have wronged myself and others. I deserve the punishment I must now receive. I declare to you, I am a man who has angered God and Man. Save me . . . help me to see the light." What a remarkable letter! Was it written after my father heard about my uncle's astronomical gambling loss? Or after my uncle had broken both legs of that French employee with his car and was forced to cough up every cent he had just so they would let him stay in Dakar?

My dad was content with his situation. He had been hired to work as a schoolteacher in the village. It was there that he met Miss Georgette. He shamelessly used to visit her at her house. He accompanied her on picnics and visits. She introduced him to her favorite books, some of which were written in French, and he could almost understand them. Although she was a Christian, she unreservedly said that his religion didn't matter to her. She was uninhibited and honest, and he loved her voice and her elegance. He had never met anyone like her. Any real knowledge of women, like Loverboy's sister—their glances, their smiles, and even their voices—was always masked behind their bodies. He never met a woman whose body did not besiege him and make everything he did difficult, as if it were happening outside of himself, outside of his own body. Georgette was definitely a different breed of woman. He was able to talk to her without feeling the weight of her body on his tongue or the weight of her body between him and his tongue. He wasn't fanatical; neither he nor his father was. Things happened quickly, though. All he had to do was speak to her, and he got very scared and was unable to sleep for two nights straight. For her part, she didn't understand what had changed in him, but she found a way to return things to how they had been. So they passed the year in a stalled relationship.

My dad was content with his situation. He was sad to lose Georgette, but she wasn't his first loss. Still, he sighed deeply, as if he were trying to breathe his way through a pregnancy. He gradually gave up reading, and after publishing two articles in a local magazine, he gave up writing. He had always been like that, ambitious to the point of torture. His life was emptied of everything but material comfort: afternoon teas, late-night escorts, and friend's houses in Tyre. He was happy because there was nothing that could wear him out before he arrived. My uncle's letters used to please him, but he never spent the remittances that accompanied them. And so he behaved like his father, who had abandoned his properties and land, happy to have banished them from his mind, who had fled his house and his town after his own father had bequeathed the family home to a younger brother in order to appease that boy's mother, his father's last wife. My father nearly fell into poverty without even noticing. Was he really like his father, unable to handle more than a single setback and yet also capable of buying the farm all at once? He wasn't exactly sure how much my uncle's loss was or how it actually came to pass. It was a burden, but my father shook it off and relied on himself. It was often said that he was a clever, eloquent man, that always remaining at the ready exhausted him, that he was honing his intelligence at every moment, was always prepared for anything. He used to get nervous before any experience, magically drawing on a power that he didn't know the source of, which allowed him to seem miraculously brilliant. It was a routine he had to stick to every day: nearly die of fear every time he didn't succeed but miraculously find power in it, converting his anxiety into ability.

Ever since he had come to the village, he didn't need all that energy. Maybe he left Georgette because he preferred not to return to that agony once again. He never made things up to his students or to the village. He effortlessly spent what he had and didn't need much to appear sneaky, as if he were up to something. The news of his brother pleased him, but he was also uninterested. His mind and his senses grew denser because he no longer cared. He wasn't upset when his sister ran off with that soldier. In fact, he couldn't find it in his heart to do anything about it. He went on sleeping a lot, without dreaming, and when he started gaining weight, it didn't bother him because that flesh accumulating on his body was none other than the embodiment of blissful apathy. The truth is that he gained a lot of weight in a short period of time. He was no longer an elegant or young man. He started to resemble those whom he used to know intimately, whose ages and bodies he refused to recognize. He was revered for his weight; it transformed him from a scrawny, emaciated boy into a full-bodied man. But that false happiness was slowly changing into exhaustion and gloomy isolation. He gradually perceived that he was lost and somewhat wasteful in this stupor, but he didn't do anything about it. He found amusing that letter from his brother, informing him that he had found his first diamond, and for the first time he was stricken with what could only be described as compassion for his brother.

In short, his appetite was diminished. He never did anything, concluding that this was his true nature and that he had no control over it. Loverboy's illness barely affected him. He went to see him in his big brass bed: skinny, splotchy, turning red with tears brought on by choking. It was impossible for him to tell things apart, and he was overcome with a desire to puke his brains out, but he was unable to expel a single particle. He had a long night, and the more he tried to get to sleep, the more his eyes hurt, the more difficult it was for him to close his eyelids. He still didn't know what he and Loverboy had actually had together. Was there something more than the amnesia of time, than lightness and absence? They had never collaborated on anything important. Still, it comforted him to be sad on

Loverboy's behalf. He found himself sorrowfully breaking down with the Judge when they heard Loverboy announce his own impending death and then laughing together when Loverboy's sister came in to finish putting on her makeup—"finger-width" eyeliner, as they used to say. The Judge had performed the marriage between Loverboy's father, the great sheikh, and the granddaughter of another great sheikh who was dead. And then he was forced to expose his backside and his legs, in the cold, motioning wickedly to my dad and Loverboy's sister.

overboy didn't die, and his sister increasingly harassed my father. This, on top of the Judge's insinuations, made my father so embarrassed that he wouldn't leave Loverboy's room because he might bump into her, as he often did as he made his way in or out. And the surprised look on his face sure was funny when he found her waiting for him in front of his room when he came out of the bathroom. She took him by the hand, and he followed her, defeated. She locked them both inside and threw him into the corner. She clung to him with her arms and mouth. She was bent on gratifying her pleasure in the short time she had before her brother noticed she was missing. When she saw that my father wasn't catching on, she took his hand and thrust it against her body. He felt his hand guided under the elastic band of her underwear. She fumbled with the buttons of his pants and had difficulty opening them. When she finally succeeded, he spurted right in the palm of her hand. As she threw him on the ground, he could hear her hiss and saw her immediately get up, smooth down her robe, and point at the buttons on his pants before she threw him out the door. Loverboy was half-asleep when my father would return to his own room. She crept up behind him and flung herself on him right in front of his bed, hunting for the buttons of his pants with one hand; he only became even more flaccid. He came again, joylessly, as if exhaling his final breath. His orgasm was melancholic, inadequate: he felt nothing else.

Nevertheless, he would always come back to find her waiting for him. Every time, in her room or against the wall of the courtyard or even in the bathroom, they went through the same routine. He would come quickly, and she would come any way she could before they parted. He noticed how much this routine seemed to turn her on even as that melancholy and inadequacy overcame him afterwards. Everyone noticed how much more beautiful she had become. The reason why didn't escape the Judge. He hinted at it often. In fact, when the Judge

63

advised him to marry her, he was really scared. He didn't sleep at all that night and resolved, from that moment, to visit Loverboy only when accompanied by the Judge. But he did return alone, and, every time, the two of them found a moment to take pleasure in one another. He would go in with a broken spirit and a broken will and come out broken down and languid. He would come in his pants and feel as though he was filling his pants with his own shit. After Loverboy recovered and was able to leave his room, my father didn't show up for any of the rendezvous she had planned for them when her brother wouldn't be around. When he noticed a young man who was known for his popularity with the ladies hanging around Loverboy's house, he got jealous but didn't do anything. He was secretly relieved because, without even trying, he had found a natural closure that saved him from further embarrassment and indecision.

My uncle's letters to him arrived. The language my uncle used—my uncle who he had previously thought illiterate—stunned him. He found that my uncle actually wrote with very few mistakes and in a flowing style that he himself never had, which spurred him to go back and reread the ancients—durable, solid, and compact to a degree that left no room for air. In one letter, my uncle announced finding his first diamond, but the letters that followed were ordinary. He didn't realize that the first diamond was meant to be savored and that he would have to wait a long time until the second one was found. He didn't know about the traditional relationships among the workers, the witch doctors, and the diamond company; a tradition in that line of work mandated that he hand over the first diamond in order to attract others. While he waited for a diamond to come along every once in a long while, the diamonds found by divers in the river or diggers along the riverbanks would be going straight to the diamond traders and, in the end, to the diamond company.

He didn't know this at the time, but he eventually understood why there was reason to be suspicious; he made certain to get his hands on a calculated, basic portion of whatever they found. He didn't know what else to do. He kicked the agents out; none of them returned the next day, and all the workers took off with them. He went to the witch doctors and the elders, but the same thing was certain to happen again; there was no way of undoing the collusion binding everyone together. My uncle nearly lost his mind and tried to kill a giant agent, who had no difficulty fighting him off. Later that evening, however, that man stole his tent and his supplies and then disappeared. My uncle often found tents stolen, probably taken by their inhabitants. Of course, his supplies would disappear along with them. He cursed those workers who abandoned him; they shouted back without bothering to look at him. They weren't workers exactly, more like thieves. They might fight each other to the death over a lousy cigarette, but they wouldn't budge in response to their boss's yelling, whose tone had become as black as their skin. No matter what he yelled, no matter what he said, theirs was a different language. He found solace in Musa, who shared not only his name, but his appearance too. They understood one another right away, and their relationship was a lot like someone talking to himself. Musa had been born in Dakar and knew everything there was to know about that place: the tribal dialects, the councils, the sheikhs, and the magic. He knew the thieves and their sheikhs, too. There wasn't a single section of this invisible web—from the lowliest workers right up to the diamond company—that he wasn't familiar with. My uncle handed everything over to him, and after one month things really started to turn around. Musa knew how to recover diamonds stolen by the sheikh's thieves before they were passed on to the diamond company. Sometimes he recovered them from the agent before they were handed over to the sheikh. In all cases, they both would have to be bribed. My uncle was surprised when diamonds started pouring in one after another. He placed everything in Musa's hands and relaxed. Sometimes he relaxed in Musa's house, the very same house where he used to stay in the guest room. He ate Sumaya's food—that sorceress of the kitchen and the best Lebanese cook in town. He enjoyed chatting with her and with her five daughters, and he started dating her oldest, Amina.

Amina was the blonde Safia had been waiting for. Beautiful, no question, quite possibly the most beautiful girl in the entire community, even if she didn't seem to know it or seem aware of her femininity at all. She freely gave her clear eyes and easy smile to anyone she saw. She also made sweet gestures: the layers of her curls, her sesame-colored arms, and on occasion, unaware of what she was doing, even her tight cleavage could be glimpsed. Her movements were all light and elegant without her even intending them to be. The boys thought she was easy, but she seemed unaffected by their insinuations. There was nothing subtle about her behavior, and she would quickly disabuse them of their double entendres and come-ons and lay them bare, like her. She didn't even wait for those who were trying to get together with her to finish their pick-up lines. She told them she was in a hurry and would continue on her way without noticing she had just destroyed something.

Wide green eyes without mystery, beauty without imperfection, and a chain of three generations of women who lived without having to rely on a man: three houses exclusively for women. Her grandmother had raised four orphans on her own after her immigrant husband died while still a young man. Her mother was raising five girls with a husband who had entrusted everything to her. Musa, so capable in the jungle, was not so in his own house. He took care of everything that didn't require words, speaking only when it was absolutely necessary. Amina had inherited her body from her father and her connections from her mother, who was not actually pretty according to how the Lebanese in Africa judged beauty. But she was, by all rights, a jinn, capable at the same time of entertaining guests, attending to her kitchen, standing beside her washing machine, and covering for Musa—who lasted only three seasons—at her neighbors' and at the evening community gatherings. She had a hundred hands and a hundred eyes. As if watching a musical comedy, her female neighbors would come up to see her water her flowers and collect her laundry because she transformed everything into a dance. Amina was like her mother, obsessed with her own private art, an art that was her whole life. She never wanted to be alone with only one person, and perhaps also like her mother she was waiting for the right time to bring this one closer to her, to bring him next to her, without ever being truly alone with him. Amina said that the time wasn't right yet, and she wasn't lying. She was in no rush. As soon as she arrived somewhere with my uncle, she immediately abandoned him, getting lost among the guests, even as Safia remained in her chair near him, noticing him from where she sat. She couldn't fathom how someone like him or like Amina could be so well known. He would give himself to anyone who passed by. She never saw him alone with any single person and didn't know to whom his whispers were directed. The blonde, the blonde who for some reason confused and enraged her by not revealing what she was so dearly holding on to, started allowing people to speculate freely about her. Safia saw her more like a sorceress. She found her kindness devilish; rather, she found her shrewd and beguiling in her exposed state. She consistently asked herself why she hated her so, and she was always disappointed to find that she had no clear answer.

Safia didn't know what she wanted from my uncle. Amina didn't even think of my uncle as a real man. She didn't think about men very often at all. As far as she was concerned, they were no lasting concern of hers. She knew that they existed and that they would appear when the time was right, when the situation required her to have one by her side.

Safia didn't know what she wanted from this man. Unlike everyone else, she considered him to be a braggart. She saw a plebeian manner in his laid-back ways. He had become quite good at addressing anyone in the same way, having nothing specific to say. He couldn't stand being alone with anyone but her, and she didn't know how to be alone with him. She had to struggle to drag him over to her house, but when the two of them finally got together, the next step would elude her. No matter what she said or did, he seemed uninterested. She would get bored and exhausted before he did, and only after she saw that he had left would she breathe freely once again, but then she felt embarrassed for what she had just done. Painful embarrassment knocked her onto the bed. She couldn't believe she was so pathetic as to try and win a man who wouldn't give her a second look. An hour later, another worry rose up inside her: *Where is he now, and who is he with?* She fully immersed herself in her anxiety and grew stiff as a board pondering that recurring question: *Where is he?* All she knew for certain was that she was clinging to this desire, which was nothing less than trying to hold on to a man whom nobody can reach. She wanted nothing more than for him to be for nobody but her. It would be enough for her just to have him nearby. It would be enough to know that he was for her and her alone and then to forget all about him, to forget about everything and return to her book, to herself. She didn't notice him when he was around; her body didn't detect him. He was barely a ghost in her life. Handsome—that's how everyone saw him. So let him be handsome and nothing more. She didn't want to try and breath from under her clothes; or, she wanted to feel his skin at her leisure. Not his scent or his touch. She wanted nothing in particular for herself and couldn't think of how she offered him anything in particular, either. Still, she desperately wanted for him to remain hers and only hers—an inexplicable desperation. For him to remain hers in a way that meant no more than that he wasn't for anybody else. She wasn't sure why she wanted to pull him away from those people she never aspired to be like in the first place— nothing more than shopkeepers and children of shopkeepers whom she, the only daughter in the house, and her mother had always made fun of.

My uncle wasn't interested in either Amina or Safia. Both of them were only twenty-seven, and my uncle didn't go out with younger women. He was certainly aware of Safia's eyes, though. He wasn't the only one to notice either. Sumaya and Amina used to tease him about it often. Safia wasn't just any young lady. She was the daughter of a man about whom no one knew anything. She had always thought that her father had feelings not unlike those unrequited feelings she had for my uncle. Sometimes she would catch him staring at her. She couldn't tell what kind of look it was, but she was almost scared for my uncle because of it. She was even more afraid that this look might have gained a kind of influence over her. Ali Sharaf was definitely not a witch doctor—she didn't care what the ignorant immigrants or the locals used to say, but she was as scared of him as they were. Like them, she felt that nothing could be kept from him. Whenever she tried to be severe or arrogant, she felt like Ali Sharaf was present, in some way, in that feeling. Ali Sharaf didn't need actually to hear her. He could read her blood. He read others' blood. Whenever my uncle visited, she knew that Ali Sharaf would show up somewhere. She wasn't surprised to see him underneath her balcony or at her front door. She couldn't read what the expression on his face was conveying to my uncle, but she could tell he was getting upset.

Safia and my uncle believed that nothing could fool Ali Sharaf, and a commonsense notion occurred to her: in some way or another, Ali Sharaf had his hand in everything. Her attraction to my uncle, to that painful power, was mixed up with her relationship to her father. This frightened her because she sometimes saw it as the source of her conflicted feelings toward my uncle. She felt it even more strongly on the night my uncle stormed out of the house, the night she believed he wasn't going to come back. She was all riled up, shouting things at him she had never dreamed of saying out loud: nobody knew where Musa had found Sumaya; no one could have any use for a mulatto woman like her except in the kitchen; Musa was crazy, and Amina was definitely his type; my uncle had never gone to school; the only people who ever laughed at his jokes were mindless merchants. She yelled and yelled and yelled. My uncle got up without saying a word. She saw him start to leave, but she let him go, simply watching the door, having lost the strength to do anything. She was running on empty when she turned around to see Ali Sharaf behind her. Without thinking, she hurried to her room, locked the door, and realized for the first time just how frightened she was. Then she found herself crying on and on, hearing her own voice as she cried, trying to keep him out, but to no avail. He burst through along with her tears. At this point, she fell into a deep sleep that lasted twenty-four hours. When she woke up, she found her door open without knowing how it got that way. She concluded that it hadn't been open for very long and that someone had left behind, in this place, something of his glance and something of his being that was still warm to the touch.

I didn't know where those useless clippings I found in four tin boxes with my father's papers were taking me. Receipts of every kind: my father's signature on the edges of some, and I vowed to reexamine each one as though I were in the throes of a Sufi *dhikr*. There were poetic commentaries, articles, a number of land deeds and official notices, all in familiarly similar styles. I didn't find anything of much interest; even the personal letters were nearly devoid of any intimacy. But I didn't give up. Not even finding nothing of interest was without meaning. I was discovering a quiet life, and I followed after it blindly. I didn't know what drove me to take out those boxes or what I needed them for. My mother was surprised to find me like that, but I didn't respond to her questions. I didn't know exactly what I was looking for. After emptying out a box, I felt even less sure of what I was after. I felt the return of a void inside me, a hunger for nothing in particular. Not even this was without meaning. Those signatures comprised some sort of last will and testament in the talismanic shape of their letters. Although I was a good reader, I read those letters without understanding what they meant. There was that frame enclosing my grandfather, fully dressed, as well as pictures of my uncle and my father on the same page. I don't know why the picture of my father seemed older than that of my uncle, why in his picture my father appeared younger than my uncle. No doubt those three pictures were taken at different times. I studied them for a long time, without moving on. It struck me that even such an unambiguous document couldn't tell me a single thing about him. There was a barrier in my mind. I needed a point of entry and maybe some kind of archaeological expertise that I lacked. I didn't hear a murmur, not even from the most recent artifacts.

I found a letter from my uncle. It was filled with supplicant expressions: "Have mercy on me. Forgive me. Help me." But even they were written in a passive voice. The weird thing was that I came across a letter from my uncle to Safia. I had no idea how my father had ended up with it. It wasn't a letter exactly, but a postcard from Marseilles announcing that he would be arriving at the end of the month. I searched for something more in the pile, but in vain. Articles my father wrote, such as "The Priorities of the Arabs," angered me as much as the letters he wrote me in that dictionary prose and formalist style that excised all the meaning, as if the meanings themselves had been cut and pasted from the dictionary. All my life, I would hear that language without getting closer to anything but his echo. Most times when I needed him, he would address me with anodyne expressions. I wanted him to be clear, to scream, to say something specific, but he didn't. His entire language was elsewhere, and I always felt that he—like his language—was elsewhere, that he never defined his own voice, not even to himself. His voice was broad, marbled, as though it were disembodied. I used to ask myself, while I observed his square chin, if he was actually present, if he was anything but a visitor to our world. I wanted him to talk to me, and I was never able to parse his tone or his language. In that moment, I felt real anger toward him, even a bit of spite. Could he actually feel pain? With the first of two antianxiety pills, his mood always relaxed. Was he truly afraid, or did he simply not understand what was happening inside, in his totality?

Such was the story of the people in my family whom I don't resemble, and even if they do believe I resemble them, they're wrong. Maybe I'm just like my mother, my mother who used to speak in clichés and slang expressions. She was afraid, too. In fact, she was more frightening than afraid. She actually felt hatred and made us feel hatred, too. What was I searching for? Why wasn't I satisfied with what I had found? Was I, I wonder, unconsciously searching for my father? I wanted him to hear me, but, once again, he didn't speak to me or else spoke in that highfalutin Samaritan jargon that made absolutely no sense to me.

My father didn't change until someone in his life died, although even then it really seemed as though nothing had happened. He married a distant cousin—somebody like the Judge's wife—who was the daughter of the mayor of a town with lots of water and trees. A marriage he wasn't ready for. All he had to do was listen to the Judge's advice and show up at a meeting that the Judge's wife had organized in their home. It wasn't love at first sight. Her kinky hair wasn't attractive that day, and there wasn't anything exceptional about her face, her eyes, or her mouth, but at least she had a face he could read. Because they were nearly the same age, their wedding was, by the standards of those days, many years late. It was obvious that no one desired her buckteeth and floppy ears. The Judge's wife tried to help make her more attractive, but her effort actually had the opposite effect because she applied colors to a face that shouldn't have been tinkered with.

In any case, this woman didn't seem to be bothered by her appearance or her age. She seemed more confident than my father, who swallowed his tongue during the meeting. Her father was a mayor, and she was accustomed to bossing everyone around at home. For that reason, she paid no attention—on the surface anyway—to age or the arrangement of the marriage. She seemed more demanding than my father and began unashamedly interrogating him, asking him about himself. The Judge's wife wanted to break the ice between the two of them, to create some mood, but my mother wouldn't allow her to ramble for very long. She turned to my father—without an introduction—and bombarded him with questions. Something about this approach upset the Judge, who couldn't stand the nerve of such brazen women. He thought she was melodramatic and told her, "You're coming on a little too strong." At first, she restrained herself from answering. It was the first time her instincts had been tested, her instincts that had always helped her tremendously. She wasn't self-conscious or tolerant, but turned insolent. Such an impression annoyed the Judge, and he told my father so. The woman didn't impress him, and his wife had nothing to say. When everyone agreed that the tension had passed, they were surprised that my father asked the Judge to ask his wife about preparations for the engagement party. The Judge didn't understand, and my father wasn't accustomed to explaining things like that.

When my dad saw his own words printed in *al-Bayan* magazine, he felt, more than anything, that those black letters would define his destiny. Until then, his life had been hard to define, but on that day he felt capable of choosing a path without running into any obstacles, without drifting too far from his own lifestyle. In his column, he used to say how the Arabic language was the origin of all regional languages—a widespread viewpoint at that time in the discourse of Arab nationalists and other nationalist sympathizers in the region. My father's interest wasn't political; his passion was in another domain—in tomes on ancient history, dictionaries, and language and grammar books. These books encrusted his eyes as he read them again and again until he could no longer tell if he was reading off the page or from straight out of his head. He tended to remember things faster than he could read them, so when he opened a book and lost himself in the page, he started by reciting from memory until he realized that he had covered many pages even though the book was still only open to page one. The truth of the matter was that he was a prisoner of his books, and in his conversations with friends or with us he would unintentionally read entire stories or sections of them out of his private memory archives.

In the end, he kept on talking like one of his books—or, that is, reciting straight from his books: he didn't utter a single expression, even to a simple shop-keeper, that wasn't culled from a book. It was hard for him to say anything he hadn't read or heard previously. He answered ordinary questions from me or my mom with an eloquent discourse articulated in such a manner that the answer was totally garbled, if there had been an answer to begin with. When the news about my uncle reached him, he began communicating his very real pain through unwieldy expressions that I didn't really understand; I couldn't tell if he was talk-ing about a camel or a human being. His eyes were desperate, confused, and at times overflowing with rare tenderness, but the language that flowed out of him always came from somewhere else. At the time, that didn't bother me, but it made conversation between us rather insubstantial because whenever he spoke to me, I felt as if he was addressing somebody else. My mother, however, considered his grandiose, dried-out talk to be a treasure, and she welcomed my dad's expres-sions as though they were sacred stones consecrated especially for her. She wasn't concerned with understanding what he said because she always considered this glorious, sonorous talk to be more than she could have ever wanted or deserved.

Safia vanished. I couldn't find her at home. Hashim morosely said that he thought she had gone to Beirut. I understood that they had had a fight, that she had taken her daughter and left. I thought she might be at Naji's; I was certain she was at Naji's. A powerful anxiety arose in me, developing at a nuclear pace. There are moments we don't believe we are capable of making it through, but I made it to that evening a survivor. I believed I could get through the night without pain, or at least with tolerable pain, something no worse than an ordinary shift at work. Even as I slept, I had no doubt that there was a period of time that had to go by, unprocessed and hollow. Still, I considered myself lucky to have made it through three days in one piece. My sleeping schedule returned to normal—sometimes I even slept more—and I happened to be half-asleep when she showed up with her daughter. She walked straight past my mother and headed for me, still in bed. Her daughter beat her there and immediately climbed up to the mirror that my uncle had made one day back when he was still a hairdresser, and she stood there, silently regarding herself. She scrunched her face up against the glass, trying to climb inside her image. There was no trace on Safia's face of the exhaustion she was pretending not to feel. She covered it up because she was classy like that. She was wearing a stunning tailored suit I had never noticed before, in which she seemed more like a lady than when she wore casual sportswear. She lifted her hair up above her shoulders—a wrapped-up body, but an exposed neck and chest. She said she could no longer stand to live with that man. She acted as if she had caught him having an affair, shouting in the loudest voice possible, perhaps to draw power away from him. *Tell me, tell me,* she repeated without waiting for my response. She carried on in that pace, with that agitation, as if urging herself upward to the height of her voice. She didn't reveal anything, and what little I could deduce from her story wasn't important. He had probably just raised his voice with her, nothing more, but she didn't want to rationalize what happened. "I've had enough," she said. "Will you come with me?" I didn't believe she meant this, but she raised her eyes to me and fell silent. "Why not?" I answered, trying to find a way out of this, but all she heard was my tone, and though I tried to take back what I had said, it was impossible to fix the situation. As she got up to collect her daughter, who had fallen asleep while gazing at her reflection, her face grew hard, and she stopped talking. She put a sheet on the couch and covered her daughter with a blanket. All of that put an end to the episode.

"It's all a mistake," she said. "First your uncle, and now this." She told me that it wasn't love, that I didn't know what I was feeling. She had said this same thing after she met my uncle. Five months had gone by, and she hadn't crossed the doorstep. She felt as if her father had brought him on her behalf. He left him on her doorstep and took off. No one knew what Ali Sharaf's intentions were or what he actually knew. When she and her mother arrived in Dakar from Casablanca, they didn't find Ali Sharaf in the palace. A little while later she found her mother in her room, unable to speak. She supposed that her father had stopped by, though her mother would never admit it. Her mother interrupted her to announce that Ali Sharaf had come in silently. He had placed the watch of the murdered servant between her legs along with his ring and his underpants, and then left. Safia had always known that the servant and the chauffeur used to bicker with one another, but not whether it was over getting into her mother's bed, whether the servant was actually an ally of her father. She decided to stay in Dakar, not to leave with her mother, but she felt unable to cross the threshold alone. For some reason, she feared that house and wasn't able to stay in it by herself. She used to hide from her father and hang out with the servants, especially dreading the garden at night, where she imagined obscure people, voices, and goings-on after sundown. After her mother's death, she slept for two days straight. Whenever she was asleep, she felt that her closed door couldn't prevent anyone who looked like her father from entering and exiting whenever he pleased. When she first met my uncle, she was afraid of him and vowed to hide from him in the palace. She thought of him as an errant bird, like her, and believed she might be able to rely on his company in order to fly away.

"It wasn't love," Safia said. "I just hesitated to leave." But in the real world, she wasn't capable of making a single move without him. Still, it wasn't love, Safia said. When he was with her, in her arms, she could tell that he didn't know how to act. He tapped his fingers and looked down at them. He was unsure where to look and didn't know what to do with his eyes. He was mournful in that moment. He mispronounced his words, nearly stammering, and a merciless lethargy overcame him. "I feel like you're insulting me," she would say, although still accepting him. She didn't say anything else. She wanted him beside her just so she could get out of her own head. Whenever they were sitting together and her father passed by, she got scared. She feared he was planning something for the two of them and that his passing by was no mere coincidence. She said she was so afraid that she couldn't even bring herself to raise her voice in her own house. Once, she got locked in the bathroom for an entire hour, but managed not to scream for help. She felt safer in there. The situation wasn't resolved until someone noticed she was missing and sent a servant to look for her. It wasn't love, Safia said, it was something more expansive than love, something that ground her down to nothingness. The more she waited for him during that period, the more she felt that she was losing her self-esteem and that at the end of the day he would find her in shreds.

He definitely walked all over her. Whenever he showed up, she screamed in his face as though he had just violated her. Sometimes, when she was in the throes of her anger, her father would pass by, making her jump as though she had committed some act that couldn't be undone. She thought he was an unforgiving man. "You want me to talk about your uncle? Take my word for it, that man couldn't spend a single minute alone." She said he never loved anyone but himself, that he was the kind of person who liked to get off in brothels, who satisfied all his vulgar needs by any means necessary. He didn't feel alive except when he was around other people. Alone, he was nothing. "But I'm not mad at him," Safia said. The time had come for her to be alone.

Hashim was another story altogether. She didn't know why she had married him in the first place. Two years passed after my uncle's death, and she had resolved to not let anyone make her wait ever again. Many didn't have the guts to look at her for the simple reason that she was Ali Sharaf's daughter. Hashim wasn't particularly brave, but he wasn't much of a thinker, either. He certainly courted her without thinking it through. He handed himself over to the diamond company without thinking. He must have known that Ali Sharaf wouldn't approve. Even his wealthy father got sick of him. Suddenly, she found him in front of her, broke and alone. The company was certainly at fault. She didn't know what hand her father had had in this situation, but she always sensed that such things couldn't be far removed from him. She couldn't figure it out, but when she found Hashim coming to her, broke and alone, she said the time was right. She simply said, "Come on, let's get married." He couldn't believe what he was hearing, but she held his hand, took him to her father, and said, with a sharp eye, "This is my husband." She saw her father, saw him standing there in disbelief, and when she repeated, "This is my husband," he was at a loss for words. His expression didn't change, but she sensed that his strength had been sapped. At that moment, she had shown him what she was capable of. It was a kind of reckoning that Ali Sharaf would never be capable of. He let her get married, and he let her go to Morocco before coming to Lebanon. He let the two of them spend money without budgets, and once again the reins of his life found their way back into his hands. She took on the burden of Hashim's loathsome qualities. She always referred to matters about which "nobody knows." Now she didn't know what she was doing: "Tell me what I should do," she kept repeating to me.

My uncle was not the kind of person who got off in a brothel, but neither was he someone who found satisfaction with the likes of Ali Sharaf. He knew that apathy in such a case came at a steep price, so he didn't remain apathetic. Anyway, young girls weren't very attractive to him, and he didn't approach Safia through her father. He was afraid of him and preferred simply to stay far away. All that mattered was that he wasn't capable of anything when confronted with Safia's stubbornness and youth. She sort of reminded him of his younger sister, who had hung on him from the moment she was born. In the end, all he knew for certain was that both his sister's marriage and her death were senseless. He loved Safia's company and took pleasure in her stubbornness, her reserves of anger, and her intelligence that sometimes frightened him. Her temper always got the better of her when she saw how amused he was by her zeal, her sensitivity, and her anger itself. To him, she was an errant bird. He couldn't believe that one day she would be part of his reality. She constantly amazed him with an intelligence he had never come across in anyone before her. Sometimes he couldn't understand her, but he felt that no one else could ever own a woman like this, maybe because she didn't own herself.

He preferred simply to listen and not to come near a young woman around whom he could no longer think of something to say. He remained silent so he wouldn't appear idiotic or ordinary when he tried to speak. She was something else in a society of petty merchants and shopkeepers. People with children tend not to have a mind for anything more than what is required to sell beads or pistachios; for the most part, their lives don't require a mind at all. It was something else, even to Amina. She brought out his feelings of academic inferiority and hidden illiteracy. The ease with which he succeeded made him feel as though there had been no obstacles to confront in the first place, but now, in front of Safia, it was as if he had to prepare for a difficult exam all over again. Under Safia's watchful eye, nothing whole remained, and every attempt devolved into a pathetic mimicking or an obvious performance—or, in the best of circumstances, a miserable maneuver. He always bit his tongue rather than dare to say something meaningless. He was born in a house that contained books, but there they ridiculed people who read newspapers in their stores, they made fun of stories, including those introduced into poetry and grammar books by Mauritanian Arabs. It was said he used to answer his African customers from behind his books without even bothering to get up. He was raised to respect books without actually reading them. Somehow a lot of information still managed to find its way into the space between his ears. Not only was Safia a reader, but she was also a writer who talked about her books all the time. In short, my uncle didn't consider himself equal to Safia or to her father's seeming omnipotence. He took care in this situation to remain a friend and only a friend to her. He saw no point in approaching Ali Sharaf, who frightened him. There was no point. Whenever Ali Sharaf appeared in the hallway, on the veranda, beneath the balcony, or in the corner of the garden, it seemed to be more than mere coincidence. It was a message or maybe a warning that time hadn't revealed the significance of yet. The time wasn't right yet, and although my uncle was certain the significance would eventually be revealed, nothing was permitted except waiting.

My uncle was happy to have found Musa, who had been born right around there, who had been raised with the Africans, and who knew them better than anyone else. He knew the sheikhs, the tribal leaders, the witch doctors, and the thieves. He was free, like them, and rarely fretted over money. My uncle gave him just about everything he had, and Musa was quickly able to placate the agents, the witch doctors, and the thieves. Work was perfect. It cost him a small fortune, but the profit was no chump change, either to my uncle, who started to live like a prince, or to Musa and his wife, who like other well-off immigrants were inclined toward secrecy in their financial affairs. No doubt the early immigrants noticed a measure of derision in my uncle's behavior, an unmistakable sign coming from the nouveau riche, who seemed to fall from the sky. What Musa pulled off was truly a miracle. The ease with which he succeeded was like a day off, like a holiday. Musa was always at work in the jungle, happy to reclaim his freedom after spending years in a stifling shop that had ended in bankruptcy and made him miserable. He was happy to spend all his time where he had grown up, alongside the people he had been raised with. He would return home only for a moment, without his or Sumaya's feeling that he had become more estranged. Sumaya had grown accustomed to his silent, absent presence. But Amina noticed. She also harbored a degree of resentment toward my uncle, who had dumped everything on Musa and left him in the jungle while he lived carefree in Dakar. Amina's secret, no doubt, was his heightened interest in her. But for the same reason she resented herself, as if by approving of my uncle's humiliation she had opened up a place for him in herself and in her house that he wouldn't give up, even when her father was around. Amina didn't understand herself there. She patiently waited for my uncle to escort her to parties and got angry if he arrived at the house early to chat with her mother, voicing his opinion and looking like a former tailor in clothes that she had laid out. Maybe she was upset because in some way it seemed as if they could forget Musa just like that; his absence didn't even seem to be noticed. She didn't like that feeling. She could tell Musa was more jealous than she had thought he was, sensing something like hatred in him that she never felt herself. It was common for Musa's entrance to be the occasion for a minor commotion, after which he would sit like an invisible creature, drinking tea in silence. Sumaya and Amina and my uncle peppered him with questions that he answered with only a few words. He might sit and review an account or a problem that was plaguing my uncle, who always trusted him. Then everyone would return to a conversation that bounced back and forth between two chatterboxes: my uncle and Sumaya.

Amina participated a little bit until she got distracted, noticing that Musa had been left in his seat, forgotten. Amina had never noticed her father's absence before. She had never missed him before. She had grown accustomed to him like that, as though she had been born to a mute father. Her father's silence and her mother's speech were interconnected to a degree that she didn't feel the house lacked speech or life. But she no longer felt like that. Ever since they had met my uncle, her father's silence had become something more specific to him: his absence. She and her father were no longer inhabiting the same place.

I don't know how Musa got in. I didn't hear him say a word. He lightly brushed by me and immediately headed toward that spot where he used to sit, on the edge of the couch, beneath the picture of my father. I didn't hear him bless my father as I expected him to. He didn't speak. When I looked over at him, I saw that his torso was stiff, that his body was nearly folded to a right angle on that couch, hands outstretched by his sides, his legs splayed out on the ground. He was leaden. His face had been strangled to the color of ivory—cruel and wooden. His deep and youthful eyes, dead in their sockets, never turned away from me. He remained in this state. I wandered off and came back to find him in the very same place. I supposed he was in some kind of trance; I had heard that on occasion he would spend hours in a single place staring at a point lost in the distance. I never heard of him going off on anyone. We were alone in the living room, and I felt that I was that vanishing point capturing his eye and that no matter what I did, I couldn't be freed from his gaze.

This feeling confounded me to the point that I no longer knew how to behave in my own body. I started to move haphazardly, as though I were afraid his stare might freeze me in place. I felt an enormous desire to get up, to walk, to leave, and never to come back to be the target of his staring, but I didn't have the nerve. We remained like this for a while, and the physical torture, which in this instance was like being made into wood, began really to affect me, even to cause me mild pain. My mother's arrival didn't change anything. His gaze remained fixed on me; he didn't turn toward her or even seem to hear her. My mother was frightened, but I calmed her with a flick of my hand. She sat down. Once her fear had melted away, she got up and left. My expression and my gestures indicated to her that she had to leave. But she stayed, as far as I could tell, in the kitchen, listening intently. Meanwhile, he remained like that, and it occurred to me, though I couldn't be certain, that the blood was gradually returning to his face, that something in him was getting ready. I was wrong. I despaired, got distracted, and then detected a choking sound coming out of his throat. He was choking on his own saliva. He wanted to speak, but his tongue wouldn't respond, as if it were a wooden spoon rattling between his teeth. He stayed like that for a moment, unsuccessfully trying to find his voice. Then he calmed down and surrendered to the silence, freeing his body from its wooden state.

My mother was at the door holding a tray of coffee she had made in spite of everything that was going on. I didn't see the point in her offering it, but the look in her eyes indicated that she could tell he wanted some. She carried the tray over to him. He reached out his hand and took a cup, but he didn't bring it to his mouth. I was concerned that in his current state he might spill the coffee all over himself, but he clung to the cup as if for some other reason than drinking. I realized that his eyes had moved from me to the cup. We stayed in that statuesque state, his eyes on the cup, my eyes on his hand, until a magical fear overwhelmed me and directed my gaze toward the inside of the cup. His breathing slowed after a bit. His body yielded, his hand brought the cup to his mouth, and his eyes began to shine. All this really took no more than a second. I asked him a question—*How are you?*—but he didn't answer right away. He seemed to be sending orders to his tongue but couldn't find his voice. His voice was raspy and coarse, and then it gradually cleared up. He started talking a mile a minute. He rambled on about a black mother and slave ships, sang in an African dialect, then shifted into formal Arabic interspersed with Qur'anic verses and well-known prayers. He laced his speech with African and French expressions. "Don't blame me, Son. I've been lost ever since that tree fell on my head," he said repeatedly. It was another version of the same old rigmarole all over again. In the end, he said he went fishing with dynamite and lost his hand in the waves. The boss had ordered him to search for it across five oceans: "Don't blame me, Son. I've been lost ever since that tree fell on my head. They gave me a new head, the head of someone I can't stand. I don't like him. I used to like him, but then I went back to hating him. Don't blame me, Son." I heard him jabber like a poet. That kernel of consciousness, that kernel of truth was present inside him. I didn't make any headway toward understanding him. He suddenly clammed up and relaxed, as if sleep or something like it were descending upon him. This was my chance to go to the bathroom, so I did, and when I came back, he had vanished.

Did the tree actually fall on him? Or had he come back to the house with a deep gash in his skull for some other reason? As soon as he had arrived, he threw himself on the ground: blood was streaming from his head, his back was cut, his knees were scraped up, and his wrists were abraded. It all seemed as if he had been tied up, whipped, and had either been forced to kneel or had fallen onto his knees, onto something rough or jagged. At home, he lay down on his stomach, and for some reason the doctor took a long time to arrive. During that time, Musa went on bleeding and raving at the same level, until his voice faded out and his bleeding stopped at exactly the same moment. What was ailing him remains a secret to this day, although Sumaya definitely preferred seeing him bleed to hearing him open his big mouth at the hospital. Amina stood beside her mother: two lost women wrapped in their robes. And as the blood started spontaneously gushing out, they grabbed each other's hands until they heard the doctor knocking on the door. The doctor told the two of them to wait outside even through he thought the wound was probably superficial and there was no serious possibility of internal bleeding. He said the two of them would have to wait, that he didn't know what Musa's mental state would be when this was over and done with.

Amina and her mother stayed up late waiting for their bloody man, whose tongue the stroke had released like never before. In that moment, a great deal of blood and a great many words came out of him, more than had come out of him in his entire life. His body and his tongue bled for a while, until they were emptied, as if nothing required medical attention any longer. A moment and then it stopped, as if there were nothing in front of it or before it. But what did come after it was blood that seemed to belong to no one and madness that seemed to belong to no one. Amina was alarmed when she saw him come in. Then, when she saw him lying before her, she felt a calm that frightened her, like the satisfaction of someone who has solved a difficult mathematical problem. The solution was right there, in that prostrate, almost alien flesh and blood. She thought of how his absence had been torturing her recently and then not at all, as if the feeling of his absence or of anyone else's didn't truly concern her. She thought her mother was no different from her, despite her concern. The two of them were so close then, so real, as if the reclining man weren't real and just being there together, embracing, holding hands were what really mattered. They stayed together like that, observing at the play of light on the wounded man's face. When dawn came, he found them both sleeping on the couch, their hands in each other's.

Did the tree actually fall on his head, as he claimed after the fact, or did five people come after him in the jungle while he was on his way home, fasten him to the tree, tie him up, and force him onto a rough branch, only to let him go after untying his hands and smacking him on the head? Or did the beating come from elsewhere? Maybe he caught it by chance while fleeing the jungle, his mind gone, paying no heed to where he was going. Was it a beating from someone close to the family? We still don't know what Musa said that night. Sumaya liked to say that a tree had fallen on him, but nobody could believe it. This outcome was clearly the fate of someone who dared to challenge the company and the thieves. Musa had paid the thieves off, but this had attracted other thieves, and the company was relentless. What happened was predictable, and it was so long in coming that even Musa started to think that maybe it wasn't going to happen after all. Still, he wouldn't have gone out into the jungle if he hadn't angered the company. Some say it wasn't an ambush. They wouldn't have needed to ambush him. They could have taken him with people around, at sunset. No one would have lifted a finger to stop them. Everybody knew them well: they were the infamous Fakk gang, from a tribe known for its tall men; some said they still ate human flesh. The workers and agents probably fled as soon as those guys showed up, abandoning Musa to them. People say that Musa ran into the jungle even after they had clamped chains on him, but they caught up with him and started wailing on him with a large bludgeon.

Nobody knows exactly what happened, and the story might have been even worse: mercenaries surrounding him somewhere and kidnaping him. Anything was possible, but the company had to have been behind it. It wasn't possible to ignore a man who claimed the diamonds all for himself; it would only encourage others to do the same. Musa must have known his attackers intimately, or else they wouldn't have been able to take him so easily. It was rare for someone to know the paths in the jungle better than he did. He knew the gang well, and maybe he even thought he'd be able to taunt them that time. It wouldn't have been difficult if the situation weren't so serious. He knew them, and the people knew them; this wasn't something that could be covered up for very long. But they went on strutting around as they pleased. No one dreamed of confronting them. That was beyond the power of the police, beyond the power of any human being.

After my uncle arrived, Sumaya locked herself in her room while Amina greeted him with a blank expression. He gathered that they both were cursing him, but he wasn't upset because he had cursed himself before either of them had a chance. No matter what, he would always be the one responsible for whatever happened to Musa. Actually, Sumaya and Amina didn't curse him any more than they cursed the jungle in which Musa had spent his childhood and adolescence with young Africans. That's how things had always been from the get-go, and they both knew there was no real reason to get upset. Still, Amina wasn't able to make peace with my uncle. She felt as if she had lost her father the moment my uncle showed up.

My uncle's situation was no better. Musa wasn't real or important to anyone else the way he was to my uncle. The blow that fell on his head was to a large extent my uncle's fate and future. Sumaya and Amina were not the only two people who treated my uncle harshly. In fact, they went easier on him than the others did. The community feared him. They were there to make money without being noticed by anyone, and his confrontation with the diamond company had unleashed the powers they feared most. The Africans also interpreted what had happened as a bad omen. The workers fled, and most of the equipment disappeared with them. The only things left standing were the huts; no one knows who conspired to torch them, but the fire spread to the edge of the jungle before being spontaneously extinguished. The Lebanese of Dakar avoided my uncle. His luck had turned in a country where everything depended on luck. The people must have seen him as bad luck. Musa, who had come out of his coma and started to roam the streets, muttering confusedly, was the poster boy of that topsy-turvy situation. Because of his newfound need for solitude, my uncle never noticed how he was always alone. He unilaterally cut himself off from everyone, even Safia, who had trouble catching up with him. On one occasion, she found him sleeping in his car right outside his front door. Of course, he was very drunk. She woke him up and told him to go to bed. He spent a lot of time in bars. Something about that lifestyle didn't suit him, so he gave it all up to spend his days in bed, grim-faced and staring at the ceiling. He couldn't get used to this either, so he went out gambling instead. When it was his turn to lose, he lost big-time. He went on losing until he had squandered a small fortune on the table. My father heard about it, went livid, and cut him off for good. He would never forgive himself for this because there wasn't enough time for him to make up for what he had done before my uncle's death. One day my uncle appeared at Musa's door. Sumaya, Amina, and the girls were at home. Musa was calm, so they sat together like they used to, but my uncle shot his mouth off, suddenly resurrecting his old self. Sumaya and Amina knew what was happening to him, so they welcomed him like an immigrant coming home again. He went home that evening feeling a way he hadn't felt ever since the accident: satisfied.

Perhaps that's when the letter I found among my dad's papers arrived. My dad's angry letter had upset my uncle very much. Their father had died the same year, and there was no one left for my uncle to write to but my dad. For that reason, my dad's letter seemed like an unappealable verdict to him. Then he regained his composure, expelled the only words left inside him, and wrote that he felt as if he owed everyone a great deal: "Forgive me." At that time, my father was up to his ears in his books. When the letter from my uncle arrived, my father was on the verge of calculating the population of Mecca during the time of the Prophet and making a map of the data. He had been consumed by the topic of false prophets, who he had discovered numbered in the tens, if not the hundreds; there was no end to them. This fact was the one thing that filled him with fear and distracted him from his other research. He assembled everything he could find out about those charlatans in a notebook that he entitled "The Encyclopedia of Errors," but he felt as if, without personally inviting the devil's hand, he had pretty much produced "The Devil's Bible." He got nervous and torched the notebook. The strange thing was that he continued to find pages from the draft of that notebook; he didn't succeed in eliminating it, or perhaps he didn't actually want to be finished with it once and for all. The other strange thing was that he also found paragraphs from "The Devil's Bible" in other notebooks, in handwriting that he found hard to believe was truly his own.

He could tell it was going to be hard for him to get out of a situation like this because such rumors could not easily be dispelled. He was confused, led astray, and might just have disappeared forever into language itself. He believed that those charlatans' siren songs wouldn't be unveiled until God himself unmasked them with His special light, His Truth. It couldn't be accomplished by human speech alone unless the lie itself was present in language, in words themselves.

There were truthful words, and there were falsehoods. He believed that truthful words were rare indeed. The falsehood splits apart and shape-shifts, accepts synonyms and adjectives, and has an array of meanings. Truthful words do not. He believed that the fixed word is truthful and that every derivation of it is a lie. But he also believed that conclusion to be overly simplistic. He believed the Book of God to be *the* authoritative source, but, fearing he might be wrong, he stopped thinking about it. One thing stuck with him, though. He thought of how language had emerged from a single word, a first word. That first word is the touchstone; every second word is less true. He couldn't resist the thought and, like a lunatic, embarked on a search for the first word, knowing full well that finding it would be impossible. It was a project that he thought was worth spending his entire life working on. He made countless diagrams. He would start with a verb and trace it to the very last possible word. That was a preliminary exploration, but it took years from his life. He found thousands of last words and didn't know what to do with them.

As I rifled through my dad's files, I found hundreds of papers with diagrams and charts and arrows and numbers. Some of them were in bags: deeds, licenses, and agreements. I'll never know if my dad had been thinking of one of those last words when the car hit him, if he heard the first word in the crunching of his bones as they were crushed beneath the wheels. This man left charts behind everywhere. Nothing had to be transferred because everything was in his charts. He compiled everything in his dictionaries—what he tasted, what he sensed, what he watched. Everything was there, everything that scared him, everything that was ever whispered to him. I tried to understand his method and to work as he did. Safia's name immediately sprang to mind. I had a mysterious desire to find her truth in the last word. I would have to reduce the words to two root letters, to derive words that were made from the addition of a third letter, and to find the ultimate word among those words, the word whose trilateral noun would not be distorted by additions. I wasn't capable of advancing even one step. The mission would require strength I didn't possess. And the simple mention of Safia's name struck a chord of nervousness in me.

Musa wandered aimlessly as my uncle haphazardly bumbled about. He was away for days on end, then appeared, only to disappear once again. Sumaya and

Amina stopped worrying about him. They both knew that he had ventured into the jungle or gone to be with the Africans he had grown up with. He was black inside, and as soon as he reconnected with his black mates, his true self would return. His obliviousness was as natural as consciousness itself; his absence was no different than his presence. Nobody there ever begrudged Nature some wandering or yelling or absence. Even his friends stopped noticing when he wasn't around. My uncle used to wander aimlessly. He wasn't the only one there who had begun with a stroke of good fortune, but was never to find a second. For many, luck came along once and then abandoned them forever. My uncle surrendered to his fate, giving in to open-ended unemployment—sleep, late nights, gambling, drinking. Amina felt, with a hint of sarcasm, that both my uncle and her father had found their own truths: being a vagabond suited her father just as unemployment suited my uncle. What really bothered Amina was her mother's situation. She noticed that her mother wasn't sleeping and that she spent her nights trying to outwit her insomnia. Amina awoke on more than one occasion to find her fumbling between rooms. Sometimes she used to find her late at night curled up on herself, taking a nap on a couch in the living room. Usually, the morning would dawn on Sumaya, exhausted, still in bed. She always woke up with a drawn face. She struggled to stick to her routine: not only did she go to sleep late, but she also began dragging her feet in doing the housework, forgetting things she never used to forget. She would gather up the clothes she hadn't finished sewing yet, neglect her thirsty plants, and sometimes even skip her morning shower. Amina noticed with disgust how Sumaya would leave her underwear on the bathroom floor. And then there was her silence, which no one was able to get used to. Amina gracefully took over her mother's work. She figured that what her mother was displaying was far less than what she was actually experiencing. She was certain that her mother would overcome her anxiety, but she was alarmed when she found a bottle of Valium among her things. That was strange in her house and in their area. Sumaya said that her neighbor had advised her to take it, but that she hadn't benefitted very much from it, so she knew her cure would have to be psychological. "'She's tired,'" she said. "'She's got five girls!'" Amina had never heard her talk like that. She had always heard her mother mock those women who consoled her for having to deal with five girls at home. It was clear to Amina that her mother was tired of herself, tired of her life. Sumaya said, "You're dad has no land, and the other one is screwing himself." *The other one?*

Why was she using such a vague title to refer to my uncle? What had placed him on her mother's tongue anyway? Amina felt as if he was still in the same place and that this time he was even more astray than her father.

My uncle cut his ties with Ali Sharaf's family, as did everyone except Musa and his family. He used to say that unemployment has more regular hours than a normal job and that being unemployed left him little time for anything else. It's possible that he completely forgot about Safia during that period, and it never occurred to him that there was anything wrong with keeping her waiting. She was unable to carry on for one more day. It was in this state that Sumaya and Amina found her at their door. She received a restrained welcome, but she noticed a startled look from Sumaya. Sumaya was behind her machine when Safia came in. She went pale when she saw her, but got a hold of herself and came out to greet her. The three of them didn't have anything to say at first, and a silence descended upon them that made Amina and Safia blush, but Sumaya remained oblivious of her guest, unable truly to be there with her. There had to be small talk, and neither Safia nor Sumaya was in the mood for that, so the burden fell on Amina, who tried repeatedly without receiving a response. In the end, she resorted to a childish ruse. She started a conversation that was irresistible there, a conversation about thieves. A reserve of stories on the topic made talking about it much easier. Talking about thieves was not so different from talking about jinns because thieves were considered a kind of magic, their actions miracles. Sumaya was the first to share news of the thieves. She couldn't resist, and as the conversation developed, she noticed the ease with which she had been sucked in and stopped. But the conversation had already happened, and Safia had participated, forgetting for a moment that she had been there to ask about my uncle. In the end, she couldn't bring herself to do it, swallowing her question every time she tried to ask. Without warning, Sumaya boorishly preempted her: "You wanna ask me about Musa? I don't see him very much." It was clear which Musa she was talking about. Safia went pale, but Amina took pity on her. "God help him," said Amina. Sumaya answered in a voice that stunned Amina, "God doesn't help those who don't help themselves." The two women were squaring off this time, with an intensity they both understood very well, but it bothered Sumaya, enough to cause her to flee that cramped triangle to the kitchen, from where she returned with coffee, only to find the two of them talking unprovocatively. And as she escorted Safia out, she found herself saying, without thinking, "Don't worry, he's fine. It's just a small crisis; it'll pass."

Sumaya had expected my uncle to show up with his eyes swollen shut and a puffy face, but when she finally saw him, she found a perfect gentleman instead. It was him. Nothing had changed. Perhaps the outbursts of arrogance over which he had no control had vanished from his eyes and his voice. He waited for her to sit down and then sat down not far from her, on the closest edge of the opposite couch. He seemed to be in good spirits, but quickly turned dispassionate, even mechanical. He asked her a lot of questions, but without any real interest. She answered him, and they spent some time exchanging fleeting, encouraging smiles. Together, they maintained a neutral and regular tone for their encounter, which didn't have, not even once, an uncomfortable moment of silence, a bow, or an awkward game played with hands and hair. She realized she wouldn't last very long in this meticulously organized space in which they had locked each other: the appearance of closeness, familiarity, and style. It was almost perfect, but there was no hope of getting out of it. To her, it was like reflection and tradition, and she suddenly lost her ability to follow. She felt a kind of quasi-physical exhaustion, almost as if she might pass out, and then fell silent. He continued but noticed after a bit that she was no longer with him. "What's up?" she asked him. He didn't answer; he noticed she was angry. "What's wrong with you?" She pushed, but he had no response. "As you can see," calmly receiving the brunt of her anger while she was in the heat of blaming him. He said he wasn't unhappy with his life, that it suited him more. "Being wealthy is so lonely," he said. "I don't do much of anything, but I'm not bored or scared. I'm losing, but I'm not scared." Her anger left her. The truly important thing was for a person not to be afraid. She knew there was nothing more important. Of course, the words he spoke weren't the words of a contented man, but those of a man who wouldn't refuse his pain or his own face. Something had certainly changed in that person, she told herself, but she couldn't quite put her finger on it—something like age or experience maybe. Perhaps it was a small lack of maturity. She could no longer ignore his understanding.

That's what Sumaya noticed, but what Amina didn't. For her, nothing about him had changed save that he had become more elegant. He seemed taller, thinner, more delicate. For the first time, Amina noticed the bags under his eyes and the trembling in his long fingers, as though she had never seen him before, as though his movements had eclipsed his appearance. She noticed the picture of his mother hanging on the wall, and it was clear how much he looked like her.

Something in him resembled the pictures, something in his silence. The picture of his mother was faded, spectral, and smudged, but Amina could discern a child in her lap whose arms and legs couldn't be held back, oozed out of his jumpsuit. That was definitely my uncle. Amina was as delighted as if she had found a drawing he had done. He was chalk white, and his face was a round circle, his cheeks floating half-circles, his mouth too. As if he were a doll. He was with his mother, who was swaddled in her veil, a paragon of motherhood. When she looked at my uncle, Amina couldn't get that image of the chubby baby out of her head. As if she had seen his soul in the picture. The more she thought about it, the more she noticed how the baby whiteness and fresh shape were still present. She laughed as she told Sumaya what she had seen, and Sumaya laughed too. Embracing him, Amina imagined herself holding that childlike creature in her own two hands. When she pointed out that picture to him, he let out a tremendous guffaw. That night, Amina dreamed of a giant naked baby with a bulging body who was laughing, laughing hard, as a woman shrouded behind her veil hurried off and disappeared. When she ran over to look at the picture, that mother had vanished. When she woke up, the dream was only paused, so that when she closed her eyes again, she had no difficulty returning to it.

Whenever she stared at my uncle like that, she discovered something irregular about him: a slightly lazy eye when he cast a sideways glance, a subtle lack of symmetry between his cheeks, two deviations in the cleft of the chin, two jutting buckteeth, a jarring twang in his voice, shoulders too narrow for someone of his height, legs too short for his torso, a limp. The truth was that she didn't stop discovering his imperfections until she realized she was exaggerating and no longer believed herself. She stopped when she realized that it had all been a game from the start. The relationship between the child in that picture and the full-grown man was, to a certain extent, something she could use to her advantage. The more the child acquired, the more she acquired. She couldn't comprehend why she adored that lack of symmetry, why she dragged her feet slowly and lazily whenever she saw him, hoping to see him limp as well. Whenever she noticed him staring out of the corner of his eye, she wished he would remain cross-eyed. Did she truly hope for that malady? Did this game have a connection, any connection, to her father's tragedy?

Amina was not the kind of woman who asked a lot of questions. Like her mother, she knew how to make useful things out of debris discarded by the side of the road. And, perhaps also like her mother, she enjoyed using her hands to make things she wanted, even improving things that she got ready made: she made beautiful covers for the radio, the chairs, the table, and the closet. She didn't know how to engage with intangible things. She knew that there were many of them—ideas in our heads, for example—but she always found something real to start with.

Amina didn't ask questions. She did a great deal. When she was certain of something, she gave up thinking about it. Once her mother had made certain that she wanted Musa for her husband, she hadn't hesitated. She had gone straight over to his house, let her hair down right in front of him, and told him to go fetch his mother. Amina thought she was capable of doing something like this, but she wasn't certain. The signs weren't there yet. Then there was also Safia. Better to wait until she was a bit farther away. The signs weren't there yet. She was waiting for the moment in which she was sure. When it arrived, she wouldn't hesitate, and at that moment neither Safia nor anyone else would be able to get in her way.

During that time, my uncle thought a lot about my father and his youngest sister, whose fate he still didn't even know. He thought a lot and replayed events and positions between him and the two of them in his mind. He revisited the violent confrontations that took place between him and my father, regretted the situation in which he had left his reckless youngest sister, subjected as she was to their father's arbitrariness. When he heard that his father had died and that my father was about to get married, he thought of sending for his oldest sister, in spite of himself. He embraced the lingering pain of his mother's death and was filled anew with an anguish that affected him as profoundly as when he had been separated from her as a small child. He spent his days unearthing this past—something that sometimes annoyed him about himself. When he finally heard of his youngest sister's death, he regretted all of his moving around. If only he'd been there, perhaps this never would have happened. Unconfirmed news of my uncle reached my father. He was annoyed that my uncle had lost everything in a single night spent gambling. He wasn't very interested in the size of the loss per se. What hurt him most was that my uncle needed to gamble at all. My father was very uncomfortable with gambling, hated cards, and anyone he saw holding them became less in his eyes. The feeling was like the humiliation his youngest sister had saddled him with, and maybe humiliation was what overcame him when my uncle died.

In any case, he kept silent, and when I poked around in my father's papers, the many language maps I found thrilled me. It seemed as though my father had created some kind of linguistic atlas. First of all, he identified continents, followed by regions, states, and capitals. It occurred to him that language can sustain a variety of climates—cold, moderate, warm. His integrated maps also pointed out parts of speech that weren't found in any of those climates. He placed those maps in a special map, provisionally calling it "The Linguistic Weather." He probably had scholarly tomes playing the roles of mediation and connection across regions and climates—or, rather, he probably had those tomes playing the roles of wind and rivers. He needed to know more about geography, having probably learned astronomy—the core of his earlier studies—wrong side up. His maps and his notes grew day after day until he almost got lost in them. Each time he felt he was approaching the First Word, he quickly pulled back, getting lost in his maps again. He was considering publishing those maps in a volume entitled *The Atlas of Language,* but he realized that pretty much no one but him would be able to decipher it. He really did float the idea by some friends, but he found it pointless. He started to write a long introduction, explaining his methods and terminology, but he found even that to be difficult. Based on his intuition and personal understanding, he used many symbols in a way that was very difficult to explain to others.

Still, he didn't give up. He believed that everything we can logically think can also be interpreted. He rejected the difficulty he was confronting, to the degree that he didn't write down anything at the time. It wasn't just a matter of understanding, but of memory. He started to record everything that crossed his mind, but upon reviewing his notebooks, he discovered that he had jumbled up unfounded ideas with others that were true. He noticed in wonder how we lie to ourselves in much of what we think and much of what we write, that we write lies without even realizing it, how we have the capacity to distinguish between lies and truth for a moment, but that we quickly abandon that capacity, forgetting what we had just realized. What troubled him even more was that he often didn't even understand the things he had written down earlier. He was stunned that he didn't get any better at reading his own handwriting, even after several tries. This was certainly reason for despair, but my father was not the type to give up; born under the sign of patience, he was constantly amazed by the ability this sign conferred, fearing that it was proof of submission or a lack of confidence.

The ability for silent fortitude would not have been a part of him if not for a real lack of anger, the lack of a spirit of resistance. My father stopped sending letters to my uncle after an unsigned letter arrived informing him that in a single night my uncle had lost enough money to buy a house.

I don't know when my father gave up on his linguistic research. Maybe he felt that my uncle's death was an indirect response to it. Maybe with my uncle's death he lost the unconscious target of his studies. He suddenly lost the site where meaning resides—the implicit standard or perhaps the world in whose equivalences he used to operate. My father integrated his linguistic maps into maps of the real world that his father had left him and that his partners had acquired. He rolled them up among his bags and boxes and pursued a single hobby at a time: first, listening to the radio, then watching television after television had arrived.

There were also unsigned letters indicating my uncle's increasingly miserable conditions. I thought about taking them to Safia. Perhaps she might know who wrote them. But Safia wasn't in the mood to look at the letters. After one glance, she said it wasn't her father's handwriting, but she apathetically pointed out how her father could have asked somebody else to write a duplicate. She was buried in her own problems and thinking about returning to Casablanca. Hashim didn't dare bother her, and she didn't complain about him. He was always available for her, but she knew that he could always do worse. He was capable of being hurtful, that she knew. Wherever he went, he would always find his way to the army officers. She knew that what attracted him to the officers wasn't just power alone. She had learned that early on, but didn't care. What she couldn't handle was his passion for being an informer. He was an informer in Dakar, Casablanca, and then here. "Don't trust him. He stings silently and can do a lot of damage." He didn't annoy her, but she got totally fed up. "Come with me to Casablanca and you'll see how great it is." The little daughter was made of stuff she had cobbled together from all over. When Safia suddenly winked at me and hugged me, I could see the little girl through her hair. She had stopped playing and seemed to observe us with contented and very wide eyes.

I showed my aunt the letter, and she displayed her amazement. She didn't distrust anyone, and when I asked her if she used to distrust Musa, she said, "God help Musa, wherever he is." I asked her about Safia, but she didn't respond at first, then suddenly exploded in anger, thrusting her nose in my face and telling me to

stop searching after things that were none of my business. "Focus on your studies," she said, "you have nothing else to worry about. Leave your uncle alone."
When I went to see Musa, he was ill. He told me he had been in bed for days. It
was difficult for me to light the gas stove, and without his instructions I wouldn't
have been able to do it. I made him tea, and he sat up in his bed to savor it. When
I showed him the letters, he took them and started to examine each one. He didn't
need his glasses. He picked up the first one and began scrutinizing every single
character so closely that I imagined he would never get through all of them. I don't
know what he was looking for, but he got lost in himself and his tea and began
moving back and forth among the three letters. This went on for a long time, and
when I noticed that his movement had become mechanical, I approached him, but
he didn't seem to notice. When I picked up two of the letters from beside him, he
noticed, but his gaze remained fixed on the letter in his hands. I asked him who
he suspected it was from, but he didn't answer, and maybe didn't even hear me.
He was like that, motionless, while I waited, until I was able to take the paper out
of his hand. I left and breathed a deep sigh of relief outside, taking pleasure in the
sky and the light. I felt as if I had escaped from something that nearly swallowed
me. Was it power that had attracted my dad and toyed with my uncle? I thought
about both of them. I thought about Loverboy and the Judge and the Poet. Illness
had recently taken the first; the second was killed in a small civil war in 1958; the
third had died of natural causes six months ago. There were no longer any sign-
posts pointing to that world of secrets except for my fear of already unwittingly
being in it.

I believed that the secret was safe with Safia, but, of course, everyone knew
a lot more than they let on. Safia was getting ready to leave for Casablanca and
finally be done with this story. Everybody blamed me because I asked questions.
Safia was determined to leave, so I no longer saw a compelling reason to keep
asking, and I stopped. But that secret, if there truly was one, devoured Musa.
He disappeared. His landlord came to me and said, "Your uncle disappeared a
month after coming home." "My uncle?" I asked him, incredulously. "He's not
my uncle." The man was impassive, much more concerned with collecting his
rent. When I told my aunt, she treated me to one of her patented outbursts of
rage. She reached a level near madness, and I couldn't bear to listen to her as she
spewed out corpses and devils of speech. When she reached the peak of her fury,
she shouted, "I told you they would burn you and eat your heart! That slut played

you!" and then, as if just noticing I was in front of her, kicked me out, "What are you doing here? Get out of my sight!"

When Musa had disappeared into the jungle the first time, Amina and Sumaya weren't too concerned because they assumed that my uncle had gone, too, along with two other people. Neither of them ever thought that Musa might get lost in an area where there wasn't a creature alive he didn't already know about. But the incident renewed their camaraderie. Musa stayed in my uncle's house for two days, bored out of his mind, until his feet carried him back outside once again. My uncle found himself in the family again. When either one of them came back, Sumaya took on responsibility for his laundry and his food, and Amina placed him entirely under her control, even taking herself over to my uncle's house. My uncle used to believe that a house with servants didn't require any cleaning, but Amina noticed neglect everywhere—on the floor, the walls, the glass, the mirrors, and the tables. But the real scandal was in the bathroom and the kitchen. She took my uncle by the hand and made him smell stenches he never knew existed in the house and made him stare down at blemishes he never realized were on his walls, his glass windows, and his furniture. When he saw what she had done, he couldn't believe his eyes. The house was a crystal, as they used to say to describe exaggerated cleanliness. He inhaled a lovely aroma and took pleasure in the gleaming, starched sheets and the clean smell. His two sisters hadn't been lazy, but they had never reached this level of commitment to cleanliness. He never knew the true smell of things or their true colors like he did that day. Something about the way Amina looked was more beautiful in the middle of that place that for a moment had a magical quality.

Safia had spent time at the house before and hadn't cared what condition it was in, so it was natural for her to be uncomfortable with Amina's behavior. Amina had become the lady of the house in the span of an hour, so Safia wasn't surprised to see her come in with a serving tray of coffee. She placed it on her knees, waiting for the coffee in the pot to cool, poured for three, and then left Safia and my uncle, and made her way home. She just imposed herself as master of the house. There was nothing that young lady couldn't do. *Who was capable of stopping her when she wanted something?* wondered Safia. Amina didn't think things over; she reacted immediately. Her body was ready. Safia didn't hate Amina; rather, she was totally embarrassed in her presence, almost to the point of losing her ability to speak. She was incapable of uttering a single comprehensible word when Amina was around. She felt a maddening density inside that she couldn't get rid of. Everything about Amina was clear and rising like the sun. She required no effort; everything was present within her. She was like a machine sometimes. My uncle, who could sense Safia's embarrassment, started to flatter her. He didn't do the same for Amina. Just the opposite—Amina began to flatter Safia, too. She used to leave my uncle to Safia and stay away from the salon when she was there. Amina liked to gaze at Safia, just sit there and listen to her even if she at times failed to understand some of what Safia was saying. My uncle angrily told Safia she was imagining things. When Amina made up her mind, no man could get in her way. Safia noticed that Amina was really keeping an eye on her. But Amina insisted that she was her friend and didn't deny Safia's silence or dryness. Safia didn't understand why Amina did that. She felt Amina had rendered her completely impotent this way. Even her anger was stripped from her temporarily. This filled her with rage toward herself and Amina. Amina's small kindnesses impeded her breathing. Safia thought she was being hunted, and she saw Amina as someone capable of killing her without betraying any sign of cunning. Safia couldn't understand what a young lady like herself, who traveled and read, could possibly mean to Amina. She was certain she didn't mean anything to the Lebanese in Dakar. She didn't believe—or rather, didn't imagine—that a young lady like Amina would look up to her as a role model. She would do anything to enter Amina's world, where she saw everything as precious and rare.

My uncle told Safia, "Leave Amina alone. It's up to her if she wants to be with someone who won't wait for her." Safia didn't need to hear this from him to understand that she had no chance of competing with Amina. But Amina wasn't underrating Safia, not even her beauty. She saw her more clearly than any man did, at times envying that almost lyrical correspondence among her voice, style, and height, that sparkle that penetrated everyone Safia looked at, the hallmark of her wide eyes, green like emerald. Amina knew that men didn't go for Safia right away, but that time was on her side. That tenderness needed the right atmosphere and spirit in order to be maintained, like a musical score, so that everyone could feel, in the end, how captivating she really was. Safia's weakness around my uncle made her not believe in Amina or herself very much. If Amina had told her what she was thinking about her, Safia might have thought that she had misjudged Amina's intelligence. But Amina felt that her feelings toward Safia also stemmed from her dissatisfaction with herself, which surprised her. She wanted to possess something that the others couldn't understand, like Safia did. That was definitely crazy. She felt it like a sickness, without necessarily despising it. Just the opposite—she loved it as she loved the numerous imperfections of Safia's body that she longed to be hers, as she loved the pronounced length of her neck, sensing something there that transcended human beauty.

My uncle told Safia she had to trust Amina—and Sumaya, too. The earring incident was not the only one, but it made things easier. Amina noticed that Safia was wearing only one earring and that she was uninterested in finding the other one. Amina looked everywhere until she found it under my uncle's bed by chance. Safia was confused, but Amina knew that the whole thing had become a kind of game. Safia noticed that she and Amina were hurting each other by their raucous joking. She was superior at using sarcasm, and it shone through, preventing her from having to show any embarrassment. She felt as though she were claiming her voice for the first time whenever Amina was around. That was the beginning of their cooperation and friendship. The two started sharing the burden of chores around the house, passing the time together as if it were nothing but an amusing annoyance. Sumaya was the real surprise. Safia hung on her as if hungering for a second mother. She needed that friendship. She felt more bound by it than she did by her relationship with my uncle. She thought that my uncle worked harder than he should have as a result of this emptiness. When Amina asked her whether she loved my uncle, she said she didn't know. Amina was surprised at her answer; she herself didn't know either. And so my uncle stopped spending time with them, but participated in their jokes and their games. In this way, the two of them felt as if they were liberating themselves from the confusion they had felt toward him. They both told him so, and he casually joined them in their game, and then they were three. What he didn't realize was that a game like that could quickly become a silk pact—a sensitive alignment that is difficult to disrupt. So every one experienced that triangle as though it were law. No one could violate it. And for that reason, it could go on for a long time.

My uncle was noticeably happier. He didn't like younger girls very much, and he felt he had reached twenty-eight years of age having already lived several lifetimes. Only a mature woman could satisfy him, even though he was still entirely clueless about sexual matters. He was forced into taking his time, which made him lazy, and on occasion into finding pleasure by simply waiting, as if stealing something from himself. He was comfortable around those two young ladies: Safia in black and white, and Amina colored in gold, white, and green. He lived in a state of perpetual bliss with the two of them, while those two young ladies enjoyed their oblivion and made competition, or should I say jealousy, into a game. One would leave an intimate trace for the other to find, and the other would keep her eye out for it until she was surprised by where she actually found it. One of them might find my uncle's underwear in her purse; or perhaps one of them might try to fool the other with a racy tale about him, the other one not knowing whether the story was true, fearing that it might not be made up. They used to straighten up his room together. Once, while they were changing the sheets, Amina said, "Why don't all three of us sleep in the same bed together?" They joined together in fantasizing and acting it out until they fell right off the bed. Sometimes, when my uncle was around, they made a series of hand gestures and winks that he didn't even try to decipher, feeling as though an entire lifetime was separating him from the two of them.

One day Amina arrived to find my aunt in the house. She was forty years old, the same age as Sumaya, dressed in a fashion that Amina found appalling— clothes that weren't suitable for anyone, no matter their age, either for lounging around the house or for going out, to say nothing of the clashing color scheme. She found my aunt skipping across a fraying carpet she had brought with her. My aunt embraced her with a warm welcome that Amina thought melodramatic. She sat down and started to make small talk while Amina looked, with disdain, at the rearranged salon. The couches and the chairs had been moved around chaotically. Vases had been taken from their places and strewn on the ground. Amina started to reorganize the room and noticed that my aunt stayed right where she was sitting, that awful bump rising up from her nose. She wasn't ugly. She had great hair—shiny, thick, and black—that cascaded onto her shoulders, but her face, covered with tiny, lentil-like husks, made Amina think of smallpox. Those bizarre clothes obscured any stature my aunt might have had, although she did seem powerful and elegant when she stood up. Without comment, my aunt left her to clean up. When she suggested they drink some coffee and Amina got up to go to the kitchen, my aunt blocked her and went herself. She couldn't stand anyone going into her kitchen; it was even more calamitous if they touched her stuff.

My aunt didn't like Amina, and she took advantage of her, asking Amina to do something for her every day. But she really hated Safia. From the moment my aunt laid eyes on her, she had understood that my father's younger brother, whom she had raised, was the one everyone desired. She couldn't' stand the young lady who arrived with a driver, politely invited her to take a tour of the city, and took her to her father's palace. My aunt took wondrous things from the palace, some of which she didn't even know how to use: the dildo that tempted her (she didn't care if Safia tried to point out that it was actually a radio part); a shoe that didn't fit her foot; large plates and knives; and Safia's mother's clothes that she found in a drawer. She took all of that, and Safia allowed her to roam at her leisure. But my aunt hated her, and because of this hatred she embellished her compliments to the point of absurdity. She used to kiss Safia every two minutes, asking her for something new each time. But she told my uncle that she was still alive and that even if he married Safia, it wouldn't make him any more successful. She was afraid of Sumaya, who was wise enough to avoid going into the kitchen. And when Sumaya learned more about my aunt's nature, she started bringing something every time she visited her. But my aunt wasn't satisfied. Sumaya's ability to manipulate people without their knowing it made her a conniver in my aunt's opinion. Sumaya reminded my aunt of my mother, whom she hated to the point of suffocation; she hated her kindness and her self-control, and she would try to provoke her with every ruse possible, but was unable to.

My aunt made friends quickly. A well-to-do relative began spending time with her, making fun of his princes and princesses. When she came back from his place, her arms were loaded down with gifts.

Amina wasn't interested in my aunt's suitor. She had bigger fish to fry. While she and Safia were in my uncle's room, Safia pretended she could smell traces of Amina in his bed. Amina really did detect a strange odor, but she told Safia, "That's your smell." There was real accusation in her voice. Her own scent: as though she were truly smelling her own body. That startled and discomforted her. She went back to Safia, and they started another game. When my uncle showed up, Amina cast him a spiteful glance.

Amina didn't know what made her so mad at my uncle. Maybe she felt he was spying on her. Her scent was on him somehow, on him without her knowing how. She was afraid. A superstitious fear of being under his power without even realizing it came over her. He was holding her scent hostage, which is like his holding her soul hostage. It wasn't possible to eliminate that intimate trace, so she kept smelling it just about everywhere in the house. It wafted by her, and she always traced it back to something that belonged to my uncle. It was on his clothes, which had become reminiscent of her. She was scared of doing laundry. That scent was all over his ubiquitous razors and towels and handkerchiefs and, of course, in his bed, which was a torture for her to make. One day, having come into contact with it, she picked up some papers she had found in his pockets, shivering where she stood, swooning a little, before thinking better of what she was doing and getting hold of herself. At one moment, she nearly felt his hair, but remembered a moment later that she had also breathed in that smell she considered hers. Naturally, she considered it hers. She never accused Safia of being a liar. She told her that it was Safia's own smell and gave up. After a while, she noticed how one typically doesn't smell oneself, but this thought didn't bother her. She was still convinced that it was her own smell. In this way, her nose and her lungs communicated with her. In this way, she spoke to herself. This upset her a little, but she wasn't afraid. It wasn't as if she were talking to herself. It was strange to find her scent far removed from her own body, but she didn't find any appalling truth in that. Just the opposite, she was happy to smell herself, as though it allowed her to know herself better. It became her little secret after Safia quit talking about it. It remained her painful game. She found herself searching after her own scent, following the faint trace like a hunting dog. She didn't know how hers could always be stronger than my uncle's. She had no reason for blaming him, but she couldn't forgive him for the condition she had ended up in. Amina wasn't one of those people who could stand transition, and for that reason she felt growing pains. This hurt her more than the wisdom tooth burrowing into her gums at the same time. She dimly believed the pain came from the same source. Amina couldn't stand transition. It was like a defect that afflicted her without her knowing how exactly. A defect in her mind or her body, she couldn't tell for sure. For that reason, she thought she was sick, that this odor was indeed hers, but that she was sick—her scent for sure, but mixed with something else that didn't belong to her. Something like maturity and experience—or rather, something like desire. In the end, it turned out to be disease, and she was afflicted.

Safia noticed Amina's absence two days later and found her at home, in bed with her dolls and the smell of bay leaves lingering in her bedroom. Amina hadn't come out once ever since she had come home, her mother said. She had shown up in shock, carrying a bundle of dried bay leaves to her room, and locked herself in. She closed her eyes in order to find strength and began searching. She had to bring her eyelids together in order to see better. She remained alone and afraid, thinking about going back. Each time sleep threatened to take her, she fought it off. She didn't know what her mind or her body was trying to do, but her body was extremely heavy, and her thoughts were too. She faced down annoying neighbors as a stormy lovesickness overwhelmed her. The illness was obscuring her path; she couldn't make it out. She submitted to being hooked up to long tubes, and the illness went away. She nearly suffocated and was repeatedly rescued and taken back to the point where she had started. She realized the futility of it all and gave in to exhaustion. But something came to her from the scent of the bay leaf, which she suddenly found and then lost. Her sight returned, as sharp as ever, her body too, but on this occasion she was powerless, as though she were being buried alive. She used to know how to find the illness in her head or in her body. She had to cut into it, to excise it one piece at a time, to erase it and watch it come back—to erase it repeatedly, until it was eliminated.

When Safia walked in on Amina, she thought her face was radiant and very beautiful. Stunned, she stared at her. What she saw was beyond comprehension. She saw Amina sleeping with a smile on her face. She was resting after having struggled for two days, finally getting what she wanted. In bed, she was beautiful, no longer a little girl. During this period, her body shook off its vestiges of childhood. That simple chubbiness in her cheeks disappeared, and her face grew into itself. Her chest filled out, and her body became stout and firm. Her body shook off its freckles; that simple sharpness in her nose and chin was evened out; the rough touch and chalky whiteness of her skin ceased to exist. It all fell out like baby teeth. She was chiseled into the bed, strong and complete. She finally emerged from the bandages. What happened over the next two days was also a celebration of maturity, or at least a dramatic farewell to childhood. When she woke up, she would find that her wisdom tooth pain had also vanished. She wouldn't feel as if anything about herself had changed. She'd be normal, more normal than ever. What will have dawned on her, without her even intentionally thinking about it, like a thought she hadn't realized was with her all along, is that she would never return to my uncle's house.

Safia saw another kind of concern written all over Sumaya's face. Safia saw her expending a great deal of energy in every movement, slow and mechanical. The coffee Sumaya had prepared for her was lacking something, and Sumaya couldn't stop herself from wallowing in long bouts of preoccupation. She didn't ask Safia about anything concerning Amina. Safia didn't tell her a thing because she wasn't certain of anything herself. The story of the scent shook her out of her reverie, but it wasn't occurring to her now. In any case, Sumaya wasn't paying attention or listening. She suddenly asked Safia, "Why don't you get married?" She said it impatiently as if she were asking her why she didn't get out. Safia was enamored of Sumaya, but at that very moment she remembered her mother and heard her kick her out of her room. Sumaya didn't return to her question, but after a pause said, "This town's got no sheikh, we want a sheikh." She said it without looking at Safia, as though she were talking to herself. It was clear that Sumaya needed more than a sheikh—maybe a god, who knows? But she went on, without any prompting, to say that she hoped to get all her daughters together and travel to Lebanon. "My dad's really old, and, you know, I don't even know my brother's wives. I'm sure they're not gonna be happy about this. Five girls, who can handle five girls?" Sumaya wasn't blaming herself or anyone else. This was her way of saying that there were things in life she couldn't handle.

I went back to digging through my father's papers. I looked again at my uncle's letter: "Save me. . . . Falsity and desires. . . . " I read it a second time and was still amazed by the strange religious vocabulary my uncle used. Where did these expressions come from? Did he write them after his huge loss at the gambling table? He didn't even tell my father about the loss; my father found out from somebody else. My uncle never told me he was in debt. This was a letter of obsession. A thought suddenly came to me and lodged in my throat: my uncle didn't write the letter.

I showed it to my mother, who claimed not to remember my uncle's handwriting, insisting that he didn't write that much anyway. But she badly wanted to tell me about the love letters my father had written to her. She had one. She showed it to me. It was written in that craggy language in which he wrote letters to me. My mother was proud of it, especially the words she couldn't understand. I noticed that the writing and the paper were unchanged by time, whereas my uncle's letter was worn and crumbling; it must have survived from a much earlier time. I had waited a long time for this letter, but then I realized it was useless. I became furious because every lead I pursued turned out to be false, sending me even farther astray. I didn't understand how the letter had wound its way into my father's papers, and I wasn't able to contact the author. My mother couldn't help;

she wasn't the kind of person who remembered handwriting, even if she never forgot a face. I don't know how this letter was received, but when my uncle's wife visited, she told me once again about how her Iraqi family had messed with my uncle's mind and talked him into marrying her. While my uncle was in Najaf for his religious education, her family planned the wedding. That was a bad omen in my mother's opinion. My mother thought this woman was harmful to his health and had afflicted him with a brain fever. She said my uncle wrote a letter to his father, the sheikh, before he fell ill, asking for his forgiveness. This was the letter that really confused me because, from far away, from Iraq, the sick religious student was screaming "Save me . . . Make me understand" in that language in which he had savored his childhood and his youth even as it was being expressed.

Amina never returned to my uncle's house. She banished him from her thoughts as though he had never existed. Even she was amazed at how quickly this could happen. She didn't anticipate that it would be so easy. She also distanced herself from Safia. She felt that she hadn't been herself all that time, that she had been playing someone else's game. She didn't have the patience to quarrel with Safia or my uncle anymore. She tried to distance herself. Safia noticed and didn't try to stop her. Her need for Amina and Sumaya was great, though, and she couldn't give that up. Amina felt as if she had changed physically, too. She was cleansing her soul and her body. She hadn't possessed anything special before—departures, appointments, family and friends. She was ridding herself of everyone, with minimal pain, without grief. She even pulled away from her mother, stopped mourning for her father, and neglected her sisters somewhat. There was a degree of harshness in that attitude, directed particularly toward her mother. She was unable to suppress her feelings of blame toward her mother, which she never fully understood. But out of everyone, the one she could least abide seeing any longer was my uncle. It amazed her to feel what seemed like resentment toward him. She was amazed at how her feelings got ahead of her. She was often surprised by her feelings; she couldn't understand how they took control of her or penetrated inside her: boredom from the others, sometimes spite and contempt, even disgust. This worried her, but she understood it could never come to pass without a certain degree of malice and secrecy, even some injury. This worried her, like a putrid smell alerting her that there was something odious about flirting with even the most attractive young men, something odious embedded in those stares and those words. Just the thought of it would cause her to lose her appetite. She recoiled as though she had tasted something rotten in her food. This game was not free of hatred. This detestable sign wasn't pleasant, but late in coming, and she had to process it quickly.

Now she had become a woman. A woman: almost the same thing as wickedness—wickedness, even as she awaited her body or was absent from herself. What Amina didn't notice was that Sumaya had also distanced herself. Sumaya had recovered from her crisis, but came back a different person altogether. She was more silent than ever. She listened carefully and spoke carefully. She behaved carefully, as if she had found something else in the other. She had lost a little bit of weight during that time, and her body started to resemble Amina's more and more: the resemblance on her face, with slight modification, would no longer be the same. Her face pulled together slightly would express something righteous in her wide eyes, her mouth moist and compact. Something that had gone unnoticed added that extra age and even extra flesh onto her, which caused her to become, a little while after the marriage, neglected. Several kilograms, just a few, she didn't even weigh herself. She had always worried so much about her figure that nothing had changed for almost twenty years. But she didn't rush to the doctor because she wasn't interested. In fact, she was ashamed of her figure for some unconscious reason, and it took her a long time to own up to that sense of shame. It all started with her clothes getting too tight for her without her at first realizing it. But what worried her even more was the fact that she could no longer bear looking at herself in the mirror. There was something like rejuvenation in other women's eyes that she was always afraid of, as if they harbored her husband or Musa in their gaze. She felt as if her skin was growing taut, as if she was concealing another odor beneath her skin, beneath the curls of her hair, but she never complained that it was illness. The doctor was a friend of hers from school—rather, he was a distant relative—and she was surprised by the way he looked at her. Something gave him pause, and he seemed to need a moment to get over whatever it was before coming back to her. The same thing happened when he raised the cover she had undressed beneath so that he could examine her. Something overtook him. He told her she wasn't suffering from an illness. Instead, he asked about her intimate relationship with her husband. He told her how her skin was lacking a nutrient found in semen. She went home utterly exhausted. She had believed just the opposite: that distance from men replenished a woman's body. She would have never dreamed that her problem had anything—not a single thing—to do with semen. She used to feel like what made her unique was the fact that her body remained her own private property, but the doctor made her see that the fact of the matter was quite the opposite.

She returned home exhausted and didn't look at her house or at her daughters. There was nothing worthwhile, nothing that would save her from the silly need for that little bit of fluid that had suddenly rendered her powerless. Two days later, she approached her husband but found him sleeping; he didn't budge after she touched him several times, so she got embarrassed and left.

Safia didn't understand why my uncle wasn't worried by Amina's absence. Even more astonishing to her was that he didn't even seem to notice. When she finally mustered up the courage to ask him about it, speech got lodged in his throat. He didn't find an answer, and perhaps in that moment he realized that he had not heard from Amina for a long time. Safia realized that nothing concerned him and that he certainly didn't notice her absence or anyone else's. She suddenly realized that he didn't notice anything that wasn't right in front of him. This frightened her, even though she felt compassion for him. She thought maybe it was just a passing phase. A passing phase—his life as nothing more than a demonstration. She didn't grieve for herself because she was too busy with Amina and Sumaya, Amina who only rarely came out of her room and Sumaya who came out often, only to go back in exhausted.

Safia usually didn't find anyone in their house, which bothered her. It was as if she had lost her family. Still, she sat and waited without getting aggravated. Once, when Sumaya returned to find Safia sleeping in a chair, something in her heart moved toward that little girl she didn't know and wasn't too inclined toward anyway, for some reason. Sumaya had the sense of family dysfunction and like her grandmother and mother before her had always know that such a day would come.

Sumaya started what seemed like a fast. She thought all the women controlled them. She wasn't afraid. She thought about herself. She thought about Safia's need for their house, but she didn't understand that it wasn't only the house that was at stake; it was Safia's need for her, for Sumaya. Safia was the first to notice Sumaya's deep transformation and good fortune. She didn't understand why Sumaya had become that way in her eyes. Sumaya thought she herself was slim and had an interesting face, got lonelier, and felt a renewed closeness to Safia after she had mustered up the courage to tell her, nervously, what had happened with the doctor. There was nobody else she could tell about this need for some nutrient found in semen, and as soon as she said it aloud, it ceased being funny.

Amina didn't think that smell would ever return to what it had been a long time ago. She wasn't very close with her mother, but the smell still affected her: a smell without quality, seemingly unreal, as if it was being discharged from memory itself. Weak but deep. She didn't quite know how to describe it. Weak but deep, as though it were being squeezed or emitted more than it ought to be able to. She didn't verify that it was actually coming from Sumaya; she couldn't be sure it was coming from anywhere at all. It sprang upon her whenever she approached something that belonged to Sumaya—her bed, her clothes, and even her hairbrushes. The smell, which was more like a whisper or even an idea, overwhelmed her. She wasn't mistaken that she noticed it whenever she came across a trace of her mother, as if she were following some undefined trace within herself. So she spent two days in a tailspin. She didn't give up until she finally started to avoid the whole mess. Even when she heard Sumaya say that she had seen my uncle on the street and that he had promised he would visit, she didn't pay much attention at first. But the thought seized her a few moments later. That was it, the smell she thought was hers when she smelled Safia on my uncle's clothes and his things.

The discovery totally opened her mind and her memory. She remembered that she smelled something like the scent of my uncle on Sumaya's clothes and on her neck. It wasn't hard to monitor Sumaya because she left her underwear wherever it fell when she got into the bathtub. Amina noticed that she occasionally came home wearing underwear marked by a powerful smell and the trace of another person's odor. Amina didn't need any more than that to be certain. She found herself unable to follow her mother when she went out. At first, it occurred to her to meet with her father. She found him wandering aimlessly, and upon seeing her, he immediately pulled himself together and led her by the hand to a nearby hill. She told him about her sisters, and when the conversation turned to her mother, it wasn't because he had asked about her. He incredulously noticed a harsh tone in the way she talked about her mother. He didn't understand, nor did he have much hope of understanding. She didn't beat around the bush, telling him flat out about her mother's long absences and her exhaustion when she returned. He looked as if he were struggling with something before suddenly going silent and zoning out completely once again. She grieved for a long time and continued to wait for his return. But that dragged on for too long. She got tired of waiting and got up to leave, at which point he raised his head and muttered nearly to himself, "Your mother, Son."

My uncle hadn't noticed anyone but Sumaya when he had entered Musa's house for the first time. She was wearing a robe that wrapped all the way around her: shoulders, chest, waist, and buttocks. It was orange, as he remembered quite well. He recalled her cheery face, her almond eyes, and especially the smile that completely rearranged her appearance and even changed the temperature in the room. In that moment, she was a she-devil, her face filled with a slight ghoulishness and longing. He had felt a balance between her laughing and her voice that was somewhere between a twang and hoarseness. She did not, however, have a pretty face. There was a thick brownness and sharp delicateness to her lips, a scar on her chin. He truly wanted to feel that scar. To plunge his finger inside it.

She had found him to be the spitting image of her husband. He didn't seem to notice that. A younger, more elegant rendition, to be sure, but still little more than a carbon copy. She had stared at her husband within him and returned to him, finding that attention, scrutiny, and closer examination made the resemblance seem even greater. The others didn't seem to notice this resemblance. No doubt they noticed it but didn't pay attention to it, which galled her even more. Sumaya had spent a third of the night going over the resemblance between the two, and she gradually grew more amazed. She asked my uncle if he had ever noticed. He said that he noticed it very well, but it didn't seem like a miracle or anything. The matter confounded her, and she couldn't think about anything else. There's little need to say that the resemblance stopped at appearances. With that exception, the two men differed. Musa was absolutely silent, whereas my uncle was always talking. For some reason, though, Sumaya had felt that the resemblance went deeper than that. Their hands looked alike and made the same things. That wasn't the only thing that united them. There was something else in their hearts and souls that hadn't become clear yet to Sumaya. My uncle was in the groove of conversation and failed to notice Sumaya when she presented him with a plate of sweets. He took a glass, looked at her, and she laughed at him. Her face turned heavenly for a moment. He felt the skin of his fingers yearning to enter her scar. She was older than he by more than ten years. In those days, that was a big enough difference for him not to be afraid. He stared at her for a second time, regained control of himself, and averted his gaze. She felt that the thing that distinguished him from the other Musa was in his eyes. The other Musa saw without looking. She felt that the difference might also be in the touch. She plunged into the conversation and talked more about what she wanted to: news of thieves.

There had been this boundary between the two of them, and each one had expected the other to respect it. There had been this boundary between the two of them, and they hadn't dared come near one another. There had been this age difference separating the two of them that they both thought was sufficient to repel any danger. They were no longer defensive, so they approached each other with a speed that frightened them both. Sumaya was the one who started the conversation by talking about her childhood, about her mother, about the orphanage for girls she had been raised in. My uncle hesitated before telling the empty "sack of meat" story, telling it for the first time in his life with details that he had always felt were left out.

They were careless together, carrying on without caution. It didn't seem as if either one of them was cautious about anything. She didn't fool herself. She never said she loved him like a brother; there was no need to. Her admiration of him and the happiness that oozed out of her whenever she was with him required no explanation. She didn't say they'd stay together at the end of the night after everyone got tired because the two of them were masters of the evening. She didn't say she'd stay up late to eat with him just because he was alone. She didn't ask. And he never asked why his feet dragged him to her place or why he always found something to talk to her about, why he would go into the kitchen with her and follow her to any room in the house just to tell her something he feared he had to say before the moment slipped away. There was no reason. All these things had happened naturally, as if it were just the way things had to be. No one had asked her why she put her hand on his arm and pushed it forward when her husband was around, why she asked him to escort her to the cinema, why she modeled her clothes for him or showed him what she had sewn, why she directed him to stores where she had found things that suited him, or why she picked out everything for his house according to her own taste. No one would ask, and a woman like Sumaya was too needy to be for just one person, or at least for one so naïve as to hide something. No one would ask. Sumaya's behavior explained some of it. It was clear enough to her and to my uncle, too. So it wasn't a bother for my uncle to bring her bottles of perfume and even jewelry from his travels, as he used to bring Musa's daughters assorted gifts. Musa wasn't the only person in the house, and my uncle often arranged to have time alone with Sumaya. He would take his naps at her house, where he had a bed, pajamas, and several razors. If he was gone for a day, they missed him more than they missed Musa, whose absence they had grown accustomed to.

When Musa got hurt, Sumaya hated my uncle. She avoided his glance and feared those feelings she didn't understand. My uncle pulled away without a sound, as if he had expected that from her. He began to count every step coming, going, to pay attention to how he behaved. Sumaya knew that if she had to blame someone for Musa's accident, then it would probably be fate. It never occurred to her to accuse my uncle, and she didn't know why she punished him or why the sight of him started to bother her, why she continued to have difficulty looking at him, why his physical presence repulsed her.

But the situation remained like that long after my uncle was gone! Sumaya suddenly realized that she no longer even had the sad result of her life, which suddenly seemed far worse to her. The ceiling had suddenly been torn off, and she—unaccustomed to fear—became afraid. She felt she had to defend every step and everything. That made her sick, and she started to lose weight. Happiness washed from her features, and when her happiness went away, they appeared more powerful and captivating than ever. My uncle wasn't the only one who was surprised. Her features weren't all that was revealed. Shapeless feelings violently assaulted her—vague memories and vaguely visible presumptions. What annoyed her even more was a grief that she felt taking its time as it wended its way through her body, rending her apart from her heels to her eyes. She was afraid, but she didn't panic. She wasn't accustomed to insomnia, but she got used to it. During those long nights, many people and faces appeared before her, but the face she expected to see was the only one that didn't appear. She was anticipating that in the end she would see what she had to see. It was just a matter of being patient, and, in fact, she did get used to it. In the end, things started to become clearer. She calmed down, as if a conflict had been resolved. In a brief moment, it was all transformed into a terrible craving that she feared her heart could not bear. She sat on the couch opposite the door, staring anxiously, relishing the taste of her heart's creation. It pained her, of course, for that to continue for days without anything happening, to feel as if she were devouring herself. Still, she remained silent and in the same place most of the time, which worried Amina most of all, but Sumaya told her she was happy—happy because she was breathing in the aroma of bay leaf, and thanks to it, she would recover.

When my uncle appeared at the door, she wouldn't budge. She let him get close to her, indicating a seat next to her with her eyes, where he sat down. She didn't speak until he appeared to despair, and when she noticed his fidgetiness, she ordered him with a single word—"Stay"—and he stayed.

He was wearing an indigo shirt. She spent some time lost in that color, breathing in the scent of bay leaves mixed with clean laundry emanating from underneath it. She also lost herself in the color and aroma of coffee. It was now possible for her to swim through any situation. Everything about that moment had its own unique happiness. My uncle didn't speak; he wasn't ready to yet, but she noticed his face clouding over, so he told her, "I'm fine." She held his hand and got lost in her own pointed fingers, the hair lying on her back, and the sweat on her belly.

My uncle had to return to sit with her for two hours every day, and she always made him stay. On the third day, she bathed in the morning, combed her hair, and waited for him in a black robe. She ordered him, "Take me to the movies."

She sat in the row closest to the screen. It wasn't hard for him to tell that she was watching without seeing. He loved rousing her with a touch of his hand; she pulled her hand back and felt the blood thumping rapidly in his hand. He felt her trembling in her seat. He waited, unsure of what to do, before he wrapped his arm around her shoulders until she gradually calmed down. He waited until she had quieted down completely and her breath had become regular once again. My uncle was scared because he had never been dependent on anyone else before. He had always lived without any interest in having a relationship, and he never took on the responsibility of another person. He was generous with his emotions, but he always gave those emotions that he had borrowed from others and not what was his to begin with. He returned from the cinema calm, but anxious about his calmness. He felt heavier than usual, as if he were on the verge of coming out of a deep sleep. He left Sumaya at the door and hurried to his house. As soon as he sat down on the couch, sleep overcame him and, after a quick nap, left him with unarticulated anxiety about some bad situation in some unknown location. It was certain to materialize as soon as he rose to his feet.

Sumaya didn't sleep for two nights straight. She went back to her room feeling liberated from an awful anxiety. She was happy about the exhaustion that had developed in her body and in her head as a result. Her thoughts and feelings were fixed on that exhaustion, that gradual recovery from the sickness that she had felt in every muscle. She felt as if her body had been liberated as well and was happy as she soaked in a joy created by the pleasure of her flesh. When she began taking her clothes off and putting them away, piece by piece, she saw her chest rising and falling beneath her nightshirt. She walked to the mirror and examined her breasts, restrained under her bra. Her skin was warm and shimmering, and her chest was heaving. She stood there for a moment, looking unsurprised, and then, without thinking, began to caress her face and neck, her stomach and legs. She did this with precision and passion and didn't leave one inch untouched. She sprawled out on her bed for a second before throwing her nightshirt back on. She put her jewelry nearby, as was her custom, but as she was taking it off, she was stricken by feelings that she was giving herself away somehow. She couldn't sleep. She didn't want to sleep. She was submerged in the smell of gas and the scent of her body. She breathed, going with herself and returning. She wasn't completely awake, nor was she thinking straight. She did nothing but take pleasure in being exhausted and in paying attention to her breathing. She wasn't fully awake as the night spread inside her, inside her body, leaving her half-dreaming, half-drunk. She wasn't asleep, but in a light that resembles dawn. Insomnia is like that—a light that resembles dawn. She didn't sleep for two entire nights—or, rather, for two whole days. She didn't know how she was able to fulfill all of her responsibilities, but when those two days had passed, she felt she had somehow regained control of her life. This feeling gave her an uneasiness that she immediately pushed away. She didn't feel desire after these periods spent deep in thought, and when she found my uncle falling over himself in front of her one week later, she kindly cared for him, treating him like she treated other patients and allowed him to disappear for another week.

My uncle couldn't remember when it happened exactly, but when it did, it happened with a staggering simplicity. She went over to his house, wearing a light jacket that she immediately threw off to reveal a translucent blouse under which her white bra could be seen wrapped around glistening, resplendent breasts. He didn't move at first; then he slid his hands over her breasts, she kept silent. She placed her hands over his and raised them to her neck. She wanted his hands to pass over her entire body. He slid his fingers inside the neckline of her blouse, and she unbuttoned it. She followed after his hands, and wherever they went, she would unbutton something: her bra, her skirt, her stockings. And once she was fully nude, she made him touch her again, from her cheeks to her mouth, from her eyes to the tips of her toes. She let him do this repeatedly, keeping her eyes closed, her breath slowing nearly to the regularity of sleep. He suddenly let out some kind of grunting noise. Her scent had intoxicated him, and her perfume spread even more powerfully as time passed, until she suddenly started dripping sweat. She got totally wet, from the hair on her head down to her feet. She got up in this state, put on her clothes one piece at a time, and left.

Sumaya listened in silence until the end. Amina waited a long time for her and then tried getting her to talk with the motion of her hand and her face, but she got no response. Nothing came out of Sumaya. She was in a position to listen, pointing her face at Amina and staring, but she was half-dead inside. Amina didn't know when she was first stricken with what seemed like a stroke. Sumaya didn't say anything. She went to bed.

After that, Sumaya went on moving and living in a quasi-mechanical way. There was something like disbelief on her face, but she hadn't even left her work. She didn't quit her job, but she had certainly checked out from her life. She would sit at her machine for hours without looking at anything but the thread passing beneath the needle. Amina would startle her by simply looking from a clock to a plant. She stopped going out and started to sleep a lot, at night and during the day. She unnerved Amina, who couldn't put up with what her revenge had led her to. She forgot about everything. She wished Sumaya would return to her old self, no matter what the cost. And when she found her sleeping, she would pass the entire day at Sumaya's machine, refusing to abandon her. Amina could see herself going out to look for my uncle in a variety of places. When she finally found him at the café, she said in a completely solid and determined voice, "Come on, my mother's sick. I want you to see her." She took him to the house. She arrived and found that her mother was no longer sitting at the machine. She kissed her and took her to her room. She chose a gown and wrapped it around her. She sprinkled her face with a little bit of powder and rolled a pencil across her eyelids. Then she put her hands on her mother's shoulders to push her toward my uncle. She left them in the living room together, feeling the weight of her decision in her bones. Without noticing or meaning to, a spiteful hatred for her father had spread inside her.

It was the first time Hashim had visited me. I was amazed that he even knew where my house was, but, then again, no one was sure what Hashim actually knew anyway. He had just sat down when without any warning he blurted out that Safia wanted to leave the country. She had told him yesterday. "And she wants to take Leila with her." He tried to seem concerned, but he was unsuccessful because he often added on a caricatured significance to everything he said or did. He had tried to assume the role of father figure, but the change in his face and the swollenness around his mouth weren't convincing. He wanted me to persuade Safia to stay. "You're the only one who can," he said. I didn't know why he had chosen me, but I certainly hoped that what he was saying about my relationship with Safia was in fact the truth.

"Sell it," Safia told me. She said she found out two days ago how he had stolen some bracelets from her. "I'm letting go so I can finally be rid of him. It doesn't matter anyway. But they're my mother's bracelets." When they had found Sara, her mother, she didn't have anything left. And yet Safia wasn't concerned about that. She said she was dead set on leaving the country and taking her daughter with her when she felt the time was right, which would be in no more than a month. She said he truly loved his daughter, but she would never entrust her to someone unemployed like him. She asked me about Musa. I said I didn't know whether they had found him yet. She absent-mindedly said she didn't think they'd ever find him. Then, looking at me, she thought better of what she had just said, exclaiming, "My God! You have his frown. Don't scowl like that; it doesn't become you at all." She shut the door, folded the sheets, and said with a stern face and a steady voice, "Come now, take me away from here."

Where had they found Sara? Safia hadn't known that they had spent two full days searching for Sara before they found her strangled to death in the jungle. Someone who had been out walking reported seeing her. It was clear that she'd been kidnapped. Her car was found somewhere else. They didn't know who was responsible. After they contacted witnesses who had spent the night with her French lover in a bar, it turned out that he had a clean alibi. Her Moroccan driver also had an airtight story because he had been visiting family. It was a well-planned crime carried out by professionals. Safia didn't find out about it right away. No one told her. When the story started going around the palace, there was no doubt that the servants, the drivers, and the kitchen staff had created a stir about it before she even found out. By the time her father came to break the news to her, she already knew. That visit was preceded by two days of absence, during which he didn't pass under her window or come near her door. Then she found him at the door. For the first time ever, she saw him discombobulated. She didn't allow him to speak, preempting him by shouting, "I know! I know! Tell me why you killed her! Why'd you kill her, why?" He turned and grabbed her as she asked again and again, screaming, "Why'd you kill her? Why'd you kill her? . . . " He didn't reply, and after a while she found herself in her room with lots of people around her, all of whom were trying, with artificial courtesy, to put her to bed. Even though she had no intentions of leaving, she felt like a prisoner in her own room. They brought her a doctor and nurses, and she understood that they were there, first and foremost, to keep her from going anywhere. She didn't leave. She was an accident just waiting to happen. All this seemed to be taking place in some distant era. She didn't feel much of anything inside. She was afraid—afraid and little else, to the point that she wouldn't dare set foot outside the door. She would shudder from a gentle breeze. The slightest wind would spread a real chill through her. She was terrified by the color of the walls, and her eyes couldn't adjust to that petroleum blue. She couldn't handle the flapping of the curtains. She was in the same pit her mother had been thrown in. Strangled, like her, or very close to the moment of her death.

The rain came pouring down, and she watched the nurses hurrying to secure the curtains all around her, obstructing her view of the trees, their waving branches and broad leaves. The rain continued to lash the window; she could hear it from inside her room. *It's trying to get in,* she told herself. *It's knocking,* she said to herself. *Those are footsteps,* she thought. The palace all around her was filled with people walking about, all trying to get in, but she was alone inside the room; they couldn't get to her. There was a magical line they were unable to cross. She closed her eyes and visualized that line. She closed her eyes. She was safe behind her eyelids, where they couldn't get in. They could knock and knock until they got tired, at which point she would no longer hear a sound from them. If they went away, she could get out of bed and stand at the fountain resting on top of the blue tile mosaic. She could see that beautiful basin hanging from the ceiling, and she wouldn't need anyone's permission if she wanted to sleep inside of it. Picture it from below: the passersby in black clothes carrying that bloated, strangled body with them. Her mother had come dressed in that African mask, feigning death in order to fool someone. Her mother and those carrying her— her servants and her drivers, her French lover—were begging to be let in. But they were going down stairs that led in only one direction: down. Down to where she would find expansive chambers carved into the rock. The rain was screaming, gnashing like the teeth of wolves. And so she retreated inside her room, safe behind her eyelids.

Safia drowned in a deep slumber. She slept for three full days before waking up. She asked for food and water, and when they came to take the plates from her, she was asleep once again. She remained in this condition for a month, sleeping and falling back to sleep, smiling and rose colored, without gaining weight or bruising her body. Then she awoke for two days, which she spent half-awake before relapsing for another month. During that time, they brought Sara's body and buried it in the garden, the garden where she had been afraid to sleep while she was alive. Sara's parents came from Casablanca and then left. My uncle visited often. Amina and Safia didn't dare to enter the palace. After Sara's death, they speculated about who had beaten up Musa and who was behind every evil that had ever befallen them.

My uncle learned of what had happened to his younger sister from my aunt. That sister was the one he had loved most in the house, and he didn't know how he could still, in that place and after all that time, grieve for her. My aunt had come, after everyone else had forgotten, to tell him that he would have to grieve on his own, that his grief would therefore be silly. He didn't know if it was even his right to grieve yet, if he was even able to cry, when there was no one around to hear his tears. He went out into the jungle alone. On the way, he flew more than he walked. He couldn't feel his feet. He just feared to stop or to arrive somewhere, as if he wanted to walk the earth on foot. He was rising above the trees, as though leaving them behind him. He put things behind him, moved on. There was not a thought in his head—just a force urging him to walk on. The rain sluiced over him, but he didn't care. Once he was soaking wet, he found he couldn't go on any farther. He stopped and at that moment felt a profound sadness. He suddenly melted into tears. He found his own way to mourn by sitting, nearly every day, next to slumbering Safia.

I enjoy imagining Musa walking the earth on foot. There are hidden imams who do nothing but walk the earth. He disappeared, and we might hear unconfirmed reports about him someday. It might be claimed that he was seen in Jerusalem or Istanbul or even back in Dakar itself. The strange thing is that none of his daughters ever called. It was even more amazing to me that when his son-in-law, Amina's husband, passed through on a brief visit, he didn't even ask about him. People said that Amina had been there two months earlier for medical treatment, but she was the last person in the world who would have been interested. My aunt found the opportunity to say how Sumaya had sought to win back her daughters' hearts. I asked her what Musa had done to deserve that. Except what was talked about, I had no idea that after his second injury, his daughters and his wife were also very hurt, so he forced them to take shelter in other people's homes on a number of occasions.

The landlord came and said, "Take your uncle's things. I have another tenant." I told him he wasn't my uncle and that I had no right to take his things. He replied, "He told me he was your uncle." My aunt informed me that although Musa had been insane, he fancied himself my uncle. I went to check out his stuff; he didn't have much, of course. I left most of it to the owner of the house so he could do with it whatever he pleased. A file under his bed caught my attention. I found pictures of women in it, the oldest of which was probably Sumaya, who hadn't become more photogenic. She is ready: her makeup, her purse, her demure posture, and her half-smile that she didn't get any better at appreciating. She is biting her lower lip, as if something startled her at the last minute, causing her gaze to stray outside the frame. A second picture of her with her five daughters assembled around her: Musa stands next to her; part of his shoulder and his body is outside the frame, and because of the back lighting, he looks as if has no eyes.

I found—to my astonishment—another letter from my father: ordinary, for no special occasion, undated. The surprising thing was the picture of an olive-skinned young lady with cheery, narrow eyes, and hair cropped closely to her cheeks. Despite her attempt to appear upbeat, a tinge of severity loomed over both sides of her face. These features didn't seem to last long before vanishing, taking shelter in another picture. It was difficult for me to find her again right away, but as I searched for her, I could imagine her in my head. It was a picture of Safia.

Did Musa fancy himself my uncle while he was mad, as my aunt said, or was it that he really couldn't tell himself apart from my uncle and that no one else could either? Not my aunt, not Safia, not Musa himself, not even my father. And what was Safia doing here? Why was her picture mixed in with his papers? I asked Safia. She said she didn't know. If there was any funny business, her father must not have been far removed from it. It turned out that she didn't know who my uncle was or who the other Musa was. The two of them had gone to Kawlakh, Senegal, together: one of them had died there, and the other had lost his mind. She didn't know who did what, but she was certain it had happened like that for a reason, that it was revenge. I didn't interrogate my aunt. I suspected that the truth would devastate her. *Leave her be,* I told myself. But I couldn't help from telling her, half-jokingly, that Musa might be my uncle. She stared back at me, and though I naturally expected her to raise her nose, she turned her face away without saying a thing.

Ali Sharaf had taken him into another room and told him, "Marry her. She needs someone." He didn't have to spell out what he meant. Here was a man who couldn't outrun his word. My uncle was waiting for this word. If he truly didn't want to hear it, he certainly wouldn't have come to it in his old age. He was beside Safia's bed, hidden away from himself, waiting for her. Ali Sharaf said that without explaining any further. He left immediately, abandoning my uncle. Safia was still sleeping, and the doctors had no hope that she would recover any time soon. But she started to get better. Sumaya said, "Marry her." Amina said the same. In fact, they all pressured him to propose. There was no other way. And Safia, Safia fell into line.

Safia didn't remember much about that era. For the most part, there they were: Safia, my uncle, Amina, and Sumaya. Everyone got back to normal. Safia recovered from her seizures. Sumaya returned as Sumaya, everyone's guide. My uncle went back to work, fully recovered from his unemployment. Musa, Musa in particular, nearly recovered from his obliviousness and went back to work alongside my uncle. Safia woke up with my uncle by her side. As she fell back to sleep, her awareness of his presence grew. Those feelings made her sleep restorative, and she slept as long as most people stay awake. She detected a pleasant scent and healing light meandering through her sleep. She found herself in Casablanca, where everything was waiting for her, where everything came to life when she drew nearer. Watching her sleep, my uncle thought her quite beautiful. Her skin was nourished, and it became full, moist, and radiant, like the touch of jasmine, and she had its fragrance too. A jasmine trellis on the balcony and on a framed door overlooking it—perhaps her dreams were flowered and scented because of that wall.

She woke up at sundown and looked at my uncle. She suddenly got out of bed and took her first step. She couldn't find her balance and didn't want to risk walking too much. Several steps separated her from my uncle, and he waited for her to reach him, as though she were a baby first learning to walk. She emerged from a dream in which she could fly long distances; now she was a prisoner of that square that was no larger than a single pace. She had to persevere, but she was terrified of overstepping her boundaries. My uncle kept watching her. She suddenly lifted her leg and balanced herself on one foot. She had only her two hands, and using both of them, she conveyed herself to him, actually arriving in his arms. Her tender, warm body was between his arms. Her porous, hollow face was stuck to his. The scent of a body returning from heaven. As he dug his hands into her waist, he felt moisture seeping between his fingers. He was filled up to his mouth with pity as he hugged her. He wasn't sure what caused him to feel this unexpected tenderness. The sight of tears in her eyes as she slept was bitter for him. He felt that the tears stuck behind his palms were coming out of her waist, out of her body; or he felt that he was hearing the tears inside his own body. She was cradled in his arms, coming out of sleep: a body prior to experience, prior to desire.

He remembered his sister and mourned her fate. He suddenly remembered the way Sumaya looked at him while he was lying on her chest. She looked at him, her body trembling inside her and inside him, as though they were filling up a geological fault together. He was surprised to remember Sumaya, but the more he remembered his own body, the more he thought about her. Safia's face was more than just that of a child; it was a witness, like Sumaya's face when she regarded him with the look of love. That really got to him, though without actually knowing for sure what emotions were being stirred up. He didn't hear Safia make a sound from over his shoulder. She stayed there, wide-eyed, looking at a plant next to the window, unthinking. The colors of the plant preoccupied her while the body clinging to her rejuvenated her. Relaxation and peace welled up inside her, freeing her from any anxiety of the moment. She collapsed on his shoulder and felt that she wasn't bearing the weight of what was left of her body anymore. Her entire weight was on top of him. It was as if the lower half of her body were floating. He remembered the time when he had taught his younger sister how to swim. He cradled her and all but carried her away. A soft night breeze passed between them and he felt that it was definitively separating them, once and for all. He continued to hold her until he felt his body becoming aroused by the touch of hers. She didn't say a word. Time passed, and the two intertwined bodies lay on each side. His thoughts were not of her when he felt her hand on his lip. She winked at him wickedly. He started to kiss her, and with every kiss she inhaled a little bit, like someone gasping for air above water.

She didn't wake up. Safia said that she lay down in my uncle's arms and that he didn't try to wake her. Their affair passed like a lingering reverie. Was it love? It was her father's wish, and she had asked all along if this engagement were anything more than reparation. She knew that Ali Sharaf couldn't harm her anymore. Her love for that ogre made her even angrier with herself, and she couldn't stop thinking about how she had remained in Dakar, abandoning her mother to her destiny. She had never loved her mother. She feared that a disaster might take place and that she wouldn't do anything about it. She didn't really want to wake up. Here was another person who brought her horror. She didn't want this engagement. She told my uncle that it was putting him in danger, but he didn't care. He wasn't even happy when over the course of two days a miracle happened: the workers, the agents, and even the stolen supplies reappeared. Musa was extremely happy and took charge of everything once again. Diamonds appeared in uncommon abundance. He and my uncle located another site for excavation. Diamonds were found everywhere, and work proceeded with clocklike precision.

Musa was extremely happy, but my uncle wasn't. He was anxious and frightened by everything that was happening. He looked at the first diamond that arrived as if he were looking at an egg, without feeling any joy. His life had changed without his realizing it. When my aunt arrived, they started bickering immediately. Each successive argument tortured him further, and through it, he was tortured for a second time by a childhood that he had spent far away, unaware. He argued with my aunt, and he was mercilessly injured by his younger sister's fate. At times, he couldn't understand why he had put himself in such a situation, why Sumaya persistently urged him to marry Safia and to get more involved in Ali Sharaf's life. The only woman he ever loved didn't want him to sacrifice himself on her behalf. She wouldn't be able to forgive herself if he had refused Ali Sharaf's proposal. Musa was the only one who was happy, who didn't fully realize the danger of the game.

My uncle spent two sleepless nights and resolved to leave Sumaya. He didn't see her for ten days. He didn't love Safia; he was with her disinterestedly. Ten days, then he found her at his door, where she had been waiting for an hour. She stared at him for a long while without knowing what to do. *It would be better for both of them if she didn't come in,* my uncle thought with both bluntness and fear that was like horror. She approached him without actually seeing him. She raised five fingers and pressed them against his face. Her fingers on his face were scary. She violently rubbed his chest with her hair and lowered her head onto his stomach, his feet, and he found her suddenly prostrate before him, raising her head to look at him with peculiar eyes. They were not the eyes of a wounded animal, but those of an animal emerging from hibernation. She was at his feet and still looking up at him when she pulled him toward her. She cast aside his shirt, the buttons of which she had torn out. She pulled him toward her with an unusual power until he leaned in. She started yanking off his clothes as if she meant to rip them, and when she saw his flesh, she craved it. Nothing could keep them apart: a nothing that swallowed them up on the floor of the room. Within seconds, a dreadful odor came surging forth like a hurricane, a hellish smell, and everything went silent, like ruins that remain standing after an earthquake. She was next to him, half-naked, and he was next to her, half-naked. Her body was inclined toward a distant place, and she entered a trance that lasted for half an hour. When she came to, she didn't move. She groaned, saying, "I'm going to die!" and got up to put her clothes on without saying good-bye. She staggered to the door and left.

I took the pictures of Musa at my uncle's grave to my aunt and hesitantly asked her, "Tell me who these are pictures of, who's sitting on the grave? Is it Musa or my uncle?" My aunt examined the picture and said, "Who sent these pictures to your dad? It wasn't me." She didn't have an answer for me. The pictures were old, the colors faded into a dull brick; the grave-sitter wasn't easy to make out because water had leaked into the picture, bleaching out parts of it. I was amazed that so much could have happened to the pictures in such a short time. When my aunt first found them, they must have been clearer. Her magnifying glass didn't help her make out the faces. She looked closely and repeated that she had never sent those pictures. Her anger swelled as she looked at them, before she blew up in my face, "What's your fucking problem? What's your fucking problem with everything? Leave these people alone, stop disturbing the dead." The tip of her nose was in my face, and I lost all hope of getting an answer. Then she abruptly relaxed and said, defeated, that she didn't know anything. She couldn't figure it out. Safia said that after Kawlakh, Musa claimed to be my uncle even though no one believed him. He came back from Kawlakh raving mad and stayed at the cemetery for a week, day and night, without leaving the grave. She said that he calmed down a little while later, but that he was still mad and didn't know who he was. One hour he claimed he was my uncle, and the next he insisted he was himself. Sumaya was the most stubborn. Safia went into a long slumber, but that's another story. Safia stayed there, talking about traveling, and one day I heard that she took off with her daughter for Casablanca without saying good-bye. Hashim didn't wait for long. It was obvious that the matter was settled in some way that pleased him.

I don't know what my father did after my uncle's death. He probably got sick from all the weeping that his body blocked and the odor coming from him that only he could smell. He came down with a terminal illness. Then one day he discovered that he had been cured without even noticing. Even more, he recovered after all those years and was finally able to cry. At the funeral for Loverboy, whom he had loved more than anyone, he felt his eyelids weighed down by tears. He considered the cure and the tears to be two final gifts from his dearly departed friend. Truly, he was cured. He was certain that his brother's tragedy had cured him. He was ashamed, but he was truly cured. His symptoms vanished along with his brother. He preferred not to think about that, not to think about anything. No, he was cured, but without any goals or any real life. He had neglected his maps and his studies, leaving himself with nothing but the television. This brought him great joy until he was crushed to death beneath a speeding Mercedes.

Now when I look back on that obsessive fascination I had for my uncle, I feel as though I was actually thinking about myself. My father was the survivor in the family, and after my own brother's death I felt that I was a survivor in the family, too, but for some reason I compared myself to my uncle and not to my father. I thought that in order to get to know my uncle, it would be enough simply to take a closer look at myself. If my brother hadn't passed away, my destiny might not have been radically altered, but it still would have changed course. That might have been the cause of even greater damage. Whatever was in store for me might have been even more terrifying, and with that, perhaps, the family's penance might finally have come to an end.

When Safia knew him, my uncle had been more circumspect. Sumaya was no longer herself, either at home or outside the house. She changed to an extent that frightened my uncle. She was convinced that there was no such thing as survival and that trying to cover up that fact was utterly futile. She felt sorry for my uncle, but she was so unstable around him that in the heat of the moment she could have thrown her kids to a wild animal without even thinking twice. My uncle had been more circumspect, but he knew that nothing could be hidden from Ali Sharaf, no matter what, and that the community was so small and showed no mercy. When Safia caught wind of what had happened, she was immediately stricken with panic. She thought of her mother's fate and was stricken with panic. She rushed to find her father in his workshop. He was sitting on a pile of iron slabs in half-darkness. She was scared at the sight of him. Although his head moved when she entered, it was swathed in darkness and appeared to be heavy, as if it had been transformed into a piece of solid metal. He stood up, and his eyes glittered. She advanced, and as she stepped forward, he vanished into the darkness. On the iron piles he seemed absent, like her, only disfigured. There was a car engine on the ground in front of her that seemed more alive than he did. She thought that if she tried to say something, he wouldn't be able to hear it. She nearly shouted at him, begging him to leave my uncle alone, whatever he decided to do. She said she didn't want him all to herself, she just wanted him alive, for him to keep on living and working. She said that what he was offering her was enough, that there was no reason to ask for anything more. She was prattling on and on, as if giving a lecture to that motor, not expecting a response. But at the climax of her speech, she heard a voice, deep and calm—she would almost go so far as to call it affectionate. The man looked at her with kind eyes and spoke in a caring tone. He didn't hold her in his arms, but he did say he wouldn't touch my uncle so long as it was her wish. He said he would leave him to his fate. *No one gets away with double-crossing me, no one*, he said. Still, he assured her that he wouldn't harm a hair on his head.

I asked my aunt how my uncle died. She told me she heard it was malpractice. They say he had some sort of pains while he was living in Kawlakh and that at the hospital they gave him someone else's pills by mistake, pills he happened to be allergic to. "Nobody knows for sure." He and Musa had gone to Kawlakh, and nobody knows what really happened. One of them came back in a coffin, and

Musa went on saying that it was my uncle; then he started only occasionally saying it was my uncle, but other times saying it was himself. In the end, he finally made up his mind by deciding to say it was he who had come back in a coffin. He continued hounding everyone until they were persuaded to send him, on account of that persistence, back to Lebanon.

Abbas Beydoun is the author of eleven collections of poetry and one novel. He is the editor of the cultural supplement of the Beirut daily newspaper *As-Safir*.

Max Weiss is a junior fellow at the Harvard Society of Fellows.